Showing Jessie

by

JoMarie DeGioia

PUBLISHED BY:

Bailey Park Publishing

I0546126

Showing Jessie

Book Five of the Cypress Corners Series

by

JoMarie DeGioia

Chapter 1

Cypress Corners, Florida

There was a naked man in Jessie Wilde's bed. Or he was nearly naked except for a pair of ratty boxers, and spread out face down as he snored loud enough to wake a drowsy alligator. One of his arms pinned her down on the mattress. Rubbing her free hand over her face, she closed her eyes and tried to rein in her anger. She could guess just how this guy got in her bed. She wasn't going to put up with this. Not anymore.

Shoving his arm off of her, she slid out from under his big body and rose with a groan. She grabbed up a quilt hanging over the iron footboard and wrapped it around herself. Though she slept in her flannel pajama pants and long-sleeve t-shirt, the March mornings were pretty chilly out by the lake.

Glancing around the tent-cabin, it was pretty easy to see that there was no one else hiding in the snug little place that had been her home for the past four weeks.

"Shannon!" She stomped as well as she could in stocking feet to the small back porch overlooking the lake. "Shannon, where are you?"

"Oh hi, sis," Shannon said, holding up a cup of coffee.

Jessie's coffee. "Want me to make you a cup?"

Jessie took in a breath and eyed her sister. Her short hair, dyed ink-black, was a mess and her eye makeup was smeared. Her clothes, garish party clothes that looked wrinkled and out of place in the light of the morning, barely covered her. It was really tough looking into that face so like her own, though. Into those big brown eyes that looked much harder than Jessie's ever did.

"Why are you out here?" she managed to ask.

Shannon shrugged. "To watch the sunrise."

"The sun rises on the other side," Jessie said, hooking a thumb over her shoulder. "Why are you out here at my lakeshore?"

"Yours?" Shannon blew out a breath. "Billy wanted to see the lake. He'd heard about Stepford and wanted a look-see."

Stepford. That was what the townies in nearby St. Cloud sometimes called the place where Jessie worked and, now, lived.

Jessie fisted her hands. "I moved out here because of just this kind of crap, Shannon. And I gave you a key to use in case of an emergency. This really doesn't qualify, does it?"

Her sister waved a hand. "Oh, relax. It's not like we did it on your bed. You were already out when we got here."

6

Showing Jessie ~ JoMarie DeGioia

Jessie thanked God for small favors. "Get your latest up out of my bed and get out."

Shannon blinked at her, and then deliberately set the coffee cup down on the decking. "Is this how you treat your only sister?"

Jessie bit her tongue to keep from telling her only sister just how she wanted to treat her. Wrapping her fingers tight around Shannon's neck came to mind.

"I'm serious, Shannon."

Shannon pouted, a practiced expression that had always worked on their late father. It wouldn't work on Jessie though. Not anymore. Shannon must have seen that, because she rolled her eyes and huffed out a breath.

"Fine." Shannon stood and adjusted the short shirt and bra top she wore, wriggling as she did so. "I wouldn't want to intrude on your precious space."

Jessie just grunted. Since when hadn't Shannon intruded on her? She was twenty-six years old, after all. Shannon was only a year younger than that. It was high time they lived apart.

"Just go?" she asked, gentling her tone.

Shannon nodded and grabbed up her huge hobo bag. "Hey, Billy," she shouted as she tromped back into the cabin in her

7

heels. "Get up."

Jessie stayed out on the deck, breathing in deeply of the cool morning air. This was one of her favorite times of the day, the early morning. The fog was lifting off of the lake in wisps and the sky was growing that pretty pink color she loved.

From somewhere behind her she could hear Billy's deep voice rumbling something or other as Shannon urged him out of the tent-cabin. Heat rose in Jessie's cheeks. She'd had enough of her sister's random hookups when they'd shared an apartment in St. Cloud, and she wouldn't put up with it out here. This was her place. Her home. If only her sister would get with the program.

Once alone, Jessie made herself a cup of coffee. The cabin was wired for electricity and had running water, but it was the gorgeous setting that drew her. Situated at the wild far lakeshore of Cypress, its only companions were ancient live oaks, towering cypress trees and the wildlife that loved the pristine lake as much as she did. Over on the main lakeshore to the west side of the property there was more development and a soft sand beach, but Jessie much preferred the wildness out here.

The furnishings were simple inside as well. Set beside the wide, decadent wrought-iron bed was a nightstand and a squat dresser with a small mirror on top. There was a tiny desk up against the bare wood framing the interior, and what she considered a quaint and rustic kitchen in the other corner. In addition to the sink and the miniscule counter, it had a small fridge, a wooden table with two chairs, and even a stacked washer and dryer unit.

She took her cup of coffee, spilled in a dollop of almond milk from the fridge, and settled in one of the chairs by the table. The tent-cabin was beginning to feel like home. She'd brought her favorite quilt from the apartment, the one her mother had done years ago with tiny pieces of cloth in faded, natural colors. There weren't a lot of her personal touches here yet, but it was a pretty cool place.

It was built of canvas and exposed wood-framed walls, and it had small windows set way up in each of the gable ends of the structure for ventilation. It was just perfect for her too, as she'd always felt stifled in the apartment. Of course, that could have been due to the company rather than the environment.

She and Shannon had lived together far too long. She knew that now. Her sister's bad boyfriend choices, her never-ending mess in their shared bathroom not to mention the kitchen made it easy for Jessie to finally make a move. Ty Walsh also helped on that end.

He was the Wildlife Technician at Cypress Corners, the place Jessie now called home. Sitting on over ten thousand sprawling acres, the property encompassed some of the prettiest land in the region. From the moment she'd toured the place with Ty, she'd been a goner. Not for him, despite the fact that he was a very good-looking guy. It was the wild and beautiful place itself that grabbed a hold of her.

It was unusual that more than half the land was set aside as a sanctuary for native plants and animals, but it made her job as a sales representative a welcome challenge. She acted as a liaison of sorts, between the Sales Center and the Cypress Institute, the body that oversaw the development's implementation of its commitment to nature. The rest of it was dedicated to expensive homes, retail stores, and award-winning recreational facilities. Jessie knew the picturesque town center and the many amenities made the sales aspect of her job a breeze, too.

There was no way she could afford a home here yet though, even in one of the more densely populated villages. Her last job had been in retail, leaving her little in the way of savings before making the leap of faith and applying at Cypress. But Ty and his wife Cassie moved out of the tent-cabin permanently two weeks ago and, when they offered it to Jessie, she gleefully moved in.

Draining her cup, she washed it in the small sink and opened her laptop. Monday was now one of her favorite days, or it was on mornings she didn't wake up with good ol' boy Billy in her bed. She slipped on her glasses and clicked her computer awake, pulling up her appointments for today. She would tour a few families throughout the day, and take one group through the wilder east side of the property in the afternoon. She was a little nervous about leading that more eco-friendly tour on her own, but Ty had told her that he had complete confidence in her.

She'd missed that kind of support since her father died, and this was another first since starting this job in June. Nine months later, she still felt flustered now and then. At least on Wednesdays she worked at the Cypress Institute all day. Research and paperwork gave her an excellent excuse to hide. From what, she wasn't going to think about right now. She wouldn't think about the who, either. Nuh uh.

By the time she drove her beloved pink Jeep to the Sales Center, she'd put aside the most recent mess with Shannon and was ready to face her day. Her father had given her the car when she'd turned sixteen, knowing she would love it. Even Shannon's birthday Miata a year later couldn't take the shine off of Jessie's Jeep.

She parked in the crushed-shell lined lot to the left of the Sales Center and cranked off the motor. Humming to herself, she brushed off her favorite cream cardigan she wouldn't need much longer this season and tucked her pink button-down into the waistband of her tan skirt. Along with her straw-wrapped wedge sandals, this outfit had become her uniform of sorts since she'd started work here. The skirt was a little bit dressier than the camp shirt and khakis she wore at the Institute.

She shouldered her thick messenger bag, turned an eye toward the coffee shop across the street, and resisted the urge to spend some of her hard-earned bucks on a caramel macchiato this morning. Lettie, that gracious, outrageous older woman who always seemed to be seated in the coffee shop courtyard, raised a hand to her and Jessie returned the greeting. Turning, she hurried into the Sales Center and ran smack into the guy she'd been hoping to avoid.

Dragging her eyes from the broad chest stretching his chambray shirt, she looked up into that perfect, golden face and forgot her own name.

***

Noah Brady reached out to grasp Jessie's slender shoulders and held her tight up against him. He could feel every inch of her

12

body, curvy and toned, but told himself he was merely being chivalrous. The girl seemed like she was about to topple over with that huge bag draped across her body.

"Oh!" she gasped, her amber eyes opened wide.

"Easy there," he said, setting her away from him with a touch of regret.

She blushed a pretty pink that did something to her eyes. Those eyes were framed in long, thick lashes he'd never really noticed before. True, he usually saw her tucked behind her desk, swallowed by the sweater she was currently wearing and hiding behind her pink-framed glasses. She was a cute thing, though. Small but loaded with those curves he'd felt seconds before. Her full lips were parted as she continued to stare up at him.

"You okay?" he asked.

She suddenly smiled, a bright expression that hit him straight in the gut. Damn, she was pretty when she smiled.

"Sure. Thanks." She stared up at him for another long second and then gave a shake of her blond head. Her soft-looking Pixie bangs fell over her brow. "See you."

She turned and hurried away from him. He stood there like an idiot, watching until she disappeared down the hallway.

"Did you need something, Noah?"

Noah turned to the woman working the front desk. Ty Walsh's mother job-shared at the Sales Center a few mornings a week, and this morning she was looking at him with an expectant expression. Sharon Walsh was a trim woman in her fifties, and Noah knew she suffered from Fibromyalgia. Ty said she had her good days and bad. Noah could guess by her bright eyes and wide smile that today was a good one.

"I'm actually here to see Ben Chapman," he told her.

Sharon nodded and turned to the computer. After typing something on the keyboard she smiled at him again. "You can go back. But since when do you ask before walking back there?"

He had no decent answer to her question. Since coming to work at Cypress back in September he'd been made to feel welcomed both at work and socially. In fact, he and Ben hung out a lot. They worked closely together, Ben as the architect in the green neighborhood of environmentally-friendly homes and Noah as the primary builder in that section. The only reason he could figure was that he'd been too stunned by holding Jessie pressed up against him.

Giving Sharon a nod of thanks, he headed down the hallway to Ben Chapman's office and rapped on the door.

"Yeah, come in," Ben called.

14

Noah found Ben poring over plans spread on his drafting table. He held a mechanical pencil in his hand.

"Working pencil and paper again?" Noah asked.

Ben shot him a grin. "I prefer pencil and paper." He ran his gaze over Noah's attire, which consisted of a thick work shirt, faded jeans and sturdy work boots. "You know. Like you prefer to get dirty on the work site."

Noah smiled. "True. We're placing footings for the big ranch-style today. Lots of footings."

Ben smirked at him. "Yeah, pal. I designed it."

Noah settled in the seat in front of Ben's vacant desk. "So are you coming out?"

"Can't. Forbes wants to see me at eleven."

"Your loss. I wanted someone there from the green side of things, though."

"Take Jessie."

Noah felt his face heat. "What?"

"She's our earth girl, right? She should be working here today, not at the Institute."

"Yeah, I saw her. But she's not a down-and-dirty kind of girl." Ben arched a brow and Noah laughed over his own words. "That's not what I meant, man."

"If you say so. Look, you're working on my designs. The Institute won't have a problem. They signed off on all the specs."

"Yeah, but I've been schooling my guys on the proper way to impact a building site. Holding extra material for repurposing. Leaving nothing behind."

"And I have to say your sites are clean. The cleanest I've seen, actually."

Pride filled him. "Thanks. This is a big job, though."

Ben gave him a deadpan expression. "Don't tell me the golden boy is nervous."

Noah chuckled at the nickname Ben had slapped on him when he'd started at Cypress back in the fall. It made him think about his surf bum days back in Melbourne Beach, but he'd grown up a lot since then. He wasn't that carefree beach boy any longer.

"All right, fine," Noah said without anger, coming to his feet. "Let me know when you want to come out and play."

Ben touched his temple with a two-finger salute and Noah left him to his pencil and paper. He passed the break room and thought about grabbing a second cup of coffee before heading out to the green neighborhood. The coffee shop was a little too froufrou for him usually, and then there was Lettie.

More than once, the southern "woman of a certain age" had all but undressed him with her eyes. She was almost always there, sitting under her crepe myrtle tree with that ever-present sweet tea in her hands.

Forgoing the drink, he left his F-150 in the parking lot and went out to the row of charged-up golf carts ready and waiting at the curb. He chose the one with nubby tires like a Gator and slid into the seat. As he maneuvered the vehicle away from the town center toward the worksite, he thought about Jessie again. There was something about her. He'd noticed it from the moment he'd met her, a coiled energy and an indefinable quality. If he had to name it, it would be closed-up. Untouchable. He wanted to, though. Just that second or two holding her close had let him feel her heat and catch her scent. Fresh and sweet, like wildflowers.

He set her from his mind as he arrived at the work site. His guys were already there. The forms were being set and he narrowed his eyes as he studied the lines. There was a lot riding on this project, both the neighborhood and the individual homes. Ben was the architect, and had been brought in not much before Noah signed with the developer to be the builder.

Noah had built a community out on the east coast, an

impressive and successful one, but this was the first time he'd worked in a place like Cypress. This particular project was only a portion of a huge development, and he could admit to himself that he was a little out of his element. He'd always preferred working with eco-friendly materials though, and here he felt comfortable making suggestions to Ben regarding the specifications of the different home models. But with the Cypress Institute involved so closely with the developer, that meant another entity had a say on just what went up in the community.

He should get with Jessie, though. Ben wasn't wrong there. She was a smart girl with an in at the Institute. Hell, she worked there one day a week. Noah had to make sure he avoided any missteps with this job. True, he'd come pretty far since nailing roofs back in college. He wasn't the only one counting on his continued success, however. No. His son Max was counting on it, too.

He switched off the golf cart motor and sat for a long minute. He wanted a different kind of future for his son. The settled, secure life he'd been working toward the past couple of years. The kind of life his parents had given him. He was tired of shuttling the kid between the boy's mother's place and his own.

18

And success in Cypress Corners would be the first, and biggest, step toward making that future now.

Chapter 2

Jessie pushed her glasses up on her nose as she studied her laptop screen. Her morning had gone by in a rush, and she was grateful to be once again tucked behind her desk. She didn't have an office in the Sales Center, but shared a large space filled with desks with Oliver and a few of the other associates. No one spent as much time in the room as she did, though. With her work for the Institute, she seemed to always have something to look up in her so-called downtime.

"Girl, what has your little nose all scrunched and wrinkled?" Oliver asked, sauntering up to her desk.

She smiled at the pretty guy. You couldn't help but, with his angel face, fair hair and sparkling blue eyes. She pushed her glasses up again.

"Just checking something out," she told him.

He sat on the edge of her desk and craned his neck to peer at her computer. "Googling anyone in particular?"

She flushed, remembering just who she'd been googling now and then since the fall. "No, wise guy. I have an eco-tour this afternoon and I want to be ready."

"You'll do great," Tammy Donato Chapman put in as she joined them.

Jessie smiled at her friend. "Thanks."

Tammy winked as she absently rubbed her baby bump. Six month's pregnant, she was still rocking her own brand of professional/sexy. Her long, dark hair was shining and her upscale business clothes fit just perfectly. "You shouldn't worry, Pixie."

Jessie shook her head at the nickname she couldn't seem to ditch since starting here. "I don't want to disappoint Ty or Dr. Robbins."

Oliver's brows arched. "Ty and the director both love you. But, there is one thing that worries me."

Jessie's heart thumped. "What?"

"Do you think you can handle the Gator?"

She knew he was half teasing, but it could be a concern. The vehicle in question, a tricked out, eight-seat, oversized golf cart with a striped canopy and a powerful motor, was well suited for the tour.

"It's not like I'm leaving the pavement," she said. "The wilder tours are Ty's thing. Besides, I can drive anything. No matter how big."

Oliver and Tammy exchanged a look and Jessie squeezed her eyes shut.

Showing Jessie ~ JoMarie DeGioia

"Kill me," she moaned.

She heard Oliver chuckling. "You're so easy."

"Shut up, Ollie." Tammy placed a hand on Jessie's shoulder and Jessie opened her eyes. "Don't let this fool spook you. You'll do great. Just tell yourself that."

Oliver gave Jessie a look of sincere encouragement, one hand splayed on his chest. "You know I tease because I love."

Jessie grinned at him. "Yes, I do."

He beamed a smile and straightened. "I have a tour in ten. Not all of us get to play in the wild today, Jessie."

She waved him away and then faced Tammy. "How are you feeling, Tammy?"

Tammy smiled. "Great, actually. The little ravioli seems to be settled in."

The little ravioli, Tammy and Ben's growing baby, looked really good on her friend.

"I'm glad."

Tammy studied her closely and Jessie stifled the urge to fidget. "Seriously, don't worry about this afternoon. You'll rock it."

Since Tammy was the number one salesperson at Cypress, Jessie took her words as high praise. "Thanks."

22

Tammy gave her shoulder a squeeze and left her to her research. Jessie hadn't worked closely with anyone before coming here, and fitting in had posed a bit of a challenge at first. Then Tammy and Oliver had taken her into their circle and she'd felt the affection missing from her life since her father passed away five years ago.

He'd been bookish like her, and had loved the environment. Loved big trucks too, though. Before getting her Jeep she'd learned to drive on his ancient Suburban. She hadn't been kidding when she'd told Ollie she could drive anything.

There was one portion of the upcoming tour she wasn't looking forward to, though. She had to drive out to the green neighborhood. As excited as she was to see Ben Chapman's incredible designs come to life, she wasn't so keen on running into the man implementing those designs again today.

Tall, sun-streaked and gorgeous, Noah Brady was everything she dreamed about. And everything she avoided. Golden guys like him weren't for her. Shannon might run through them like Kleenex but Jessie? She'd been easy prey for that kind of guy right after her father died, a super smart grad student who'd taken pleasure in dominating her. And no matter what she gave up in her quest to satisfy him, he still ended up hurting her. As it turned out, she couldn't be enough for him.

After eating a yogurt in the break room, she grabbed a bottle of water and went out to the lobby to wait for her tour group. Dr. Robbins had told her they were mostly in the "Active Adult" stage of their lives, so she anticipated a tame tour. They were very keen on the green aspects too, so she would drive them out to where the concrete raceways would be built for the algae fields. Part of her research this morning was on just that. The Institute was still looking into logistics, which meant lots of meetings with Mr. Forbes and Dr. Robbins. And she was happily stuck between the developer and the director.

Information was like her crack. She could lose herself in numbers and statistics, but she would talk in laymen's terms during today's tour. That was the reason Mr. Forbes let her work so closely with the Institute. He'd told her time and again that residents and visitors both responded to her excitement and enthusiasm. She wasn't sure about that, but she did feel most comfortable when she was speaking on a well-researched topic. Go figure.

It had warmed up since this morning, so she'd left her sweater on the back of her chair and now the A/C in the Sales Center caused the skin on her arms to raise in goosebumps.

Two couples waited for her in the lobby, and she felt that flutter of nervousness again. Planting a smile on her face, she approached them.

"Good afternoon," she said. "I'm Jessie."

The four people returned the expression as they all chimed in with their greetings. Each couple, one pair on the taller side, was a matched set and neat in their pressed resort wear. Once more she was grateful she wouldn't be leaving the pavement today. The ride might rumple their crisp linen pants and muss their silvery hair, but she'd do her best to keep them safe otherwise.

"I've been so looking forward to this," the taller woman gushed. "Tammy said you're just the one for this tour, though I admit I'm a little bit nervous."

Jessie caught Sharon Walsh's wink and thumbs-up from the front desk, and her own smile felt less forced now. "I promise to bring all of us back alive," she assured them.

The men laughed and the two older women shared an expression of relief.

Jessie squared her shoulders. "Shall we go?"

They all murmured their agreement and she waved them ahead of her into the sunshine. It was a beautiful spring afternoon and, although the temperature had climbed since the morning, there was a breeze in the air that would kick up as they rode over the property.

"I thought we'd start by heading east," she said as they buckled into their seats of the Gator.

"Is it as wild as Tammy said?" the shorter woman asked.

Jessie nodded. "Yes, but we're not going to off-road today. We'll probably see some wildlife along the way, though."

They all shifted in their seats as Jessie drove them out to the less developed part of Cypress. As they made their way, she warmed to her topic and gave them some of the particulars that she only touched on during her regular tours for prospective residents.

The drive out to the east side was one of her favorites, and one she made every day now. Her own piece of serenity was set just to the left as they rounded a curve.

"What's that little structure down that sandy path?" one of the men asked.

Jessie felt a flush of pleasure as she answered. "That's my tent-cabin."

"You live out here?" the tall woman asked. "By yourself?"

"I do," Jessie said.

"Don't you get lonely?" the other woman asked.

The question drew Jessie up short. She didn't miss living with Shannon, but she did miss having another heartbeat in the house. She hadn't had a pet since she was a teenager, and there were tons of heartbeats just outside her new home. Not that she'd invite any of those animals in to cuddle in that wide, empty bed.

"I like the peace and quiet," was all she would say. It was part of the truth, anyway.

Her four guests appeared to take her answer at face value, so she gave a sharp nod and continued the tour.

"How many of you have heard of biofuel?" she asked.

The men both said they'd read about it or heard about it on TV, so she kept her spiel on the basic side.

"Both the Cypress Institute and the developer are working on the logistics of setting aside some land for algae fields," she began.

"How much land?" the shorter man asked.

"Up to fifty acres."

"That's not much," the tall woman said. "Is it?"

Jessie smiled over her shoulder at her. "Not in the grand scheme of things. Cypress sits on over ten thousand acres, but more than half of that is reserved for conservation. The concrete raceways, the controlled ponds for algae growth, wouldn't be in anyone's way out here."

"When would they start building?" the shorter man asked.

"Not for a few years yet," Jessie told him. "It's exciting to think about Cypress starting to provide some of its own energy, though."

She could almost feel their minds working as they absorbed everything she told them. Caught up in her presentation, she breezed through the rest of the tour and soon found herself driving through the town center. Trepidation made her nerves zing a little bit.

"Now we'll see the homes in the green neighborhood," she managed to say.

"Are they all green?" one of the men quipped.

She chuckled. "To their studs."

"Ooh, studs," one of the women laughed.

Jessie smiled but her mind turned immediately to one particular stud. Oh God, she might have to see Noah again. Maybe not, though. Maybe he'd be too busy on the new construction to be hanging around the model homes.

Shoving the delectable image of him in his soft and sturdy-looking work clothes out of her mind, she returned to her spiel.

"Part of today's tour involves a walk through one of the models Ben Chapman designed. It features many earth-friendly materials yet is gorgeous and very comfortable."

"Sounds good," one of the men said.

"If I had a dream house in mind, it would be situated on this particular piece of land," Jessie said. "Homes both large and small will fill the neighborhood when it's complete."

"When will that be?" the tall woman asked.

"In about two years the first phase will be occupied. About thirty larger homes and fifty on a smaller scale."

"And this is the first phase?" the tall man asked.

"Yes," Jessie said. "There's a lot riding on the feasibility of an entire neighborhood built with an eye to ecology."

"And a lot of money, I bet," the man put in.

"That's why there will be homes of varying sizes and price points," Jessie said. "People of different budgets and home needs might still share the same enthusiasm for living green."

They grew quiet again, apparently mulling over all she'd told them this afternoon. Pulling the Gator up to the curb near the two-story model, she cranked off the motor and swiveled to face her guests.

"Here's the model I wanted to show you all," she said with a smile. "It's a great example of living comfortably green."

She stepped out onto the pavement and waited for her group to do likewise. When the two women began to ooh and ahh she turned to follow their line of sight, fully prepared to fan the flames of their admiration for the impressive home. Instead, she saw Noah standing on the porch, leaning on one column with his long legs crossed at the ankles.

"Hey there, Jessie," he said, his husky voice reaching her.

She gaped at him for a beat, taking him in from the top of his tousled sun-kissed hair to his big booted feet. Oh, he looked so darn good. Talk about a dream. She could only imagine having him to come home to.

"What was that about studs, dear?" one of the women teased from behind.

Her face flaming, Jessie dragged her gaze from the magnificent male specimen on display to the sidewalk beneath her wedges. So much for avoiding him.

Crap.

***

Noah caught the pretty blush of pink on Jessie's cheeks even from where he stood, and couldn't help but grin. She was so

30

damn cute, and a little bit mussed from her tour in the open Gator. Her short blond hair was a cloud she attempted to smooth down as she approached the model home with obvious reluctance. Her companions weren't so shy. They were two older couples, smiling and talking as they stepped out of the Gator. They seemed very excited to tour the model, too.

He stepped down and greeted them. "Hi. I'm Noah Brady, the builder in this community."

The four of them appeared impressed, which was a common reaction when he told people that. He was proud of his work, but he wasn't going to take credit for either Ben's designs or the developer's setting.

"This neighborhood is going to be beautiful," the shorter woman said.

"Ben Chapman is a gifted architect," he told them.

"And your work is bringing it all to life," Jessie said.

He caught her eyes, bare of her glasses again. The rich coffee color was mixed with gold right now, and swirled with something he couldn't decipher. When those eyes flicked over him again, a punch of lust hit him square in the gut.

"Just doing my job," he said with a smile.

She dipped her head as she passed him, turning her attention to her tour group. "Let's go inside."

He stepped back and watched as she led them into the house. He wanted to follow, if only to watch her ass wriggle as she walked on those sandals, but he didn't have any excuse to linger.

As the sound of her voice reached him, explaining and pointing out the many eco-friendly and high-end features of the house, he headed back out to his work site six lots over. The footings were set now, the concrete poured, and there were only a couple of guys still onsite. The day was winding down and he wanted to touch base with his project supervisor.

"Hey, boss," the supervisor called.

Noah lifted his hand in a wave. "Hey, Mike."

Mike pulled an envelope out of his pocket. "The inspector signed off on the footings."

"He was here already?"

"Yep."

Noah nodded as he took the documents. "Good. I'll arrange for the concrete blocks for the stem wall."

Mike nodded. "I'll get with the crew and have everybody here. Just text me the time."

"Will do." Noah fist-bumped Mike. "Thanks, man."

Noah slipped a copy of the approval into the permit box set on a post in front of the lot and then pulled out his phone. He made a quick call to his block supplier to confirm his order for the stem wall and scheduled delivery for the next morning. After texting Mike the info, he got into the golf cart and headed back to the town center.

Work was progressing on this project, and the now-familiar adrenaline filled him. He'd built six houses here in the neighborhood so far, and a handful of families had already taken occupancy.

Ben and his wife lived in the two-story Craftsman style that had originally been planned as model, but there was another of that design slated to be built after this oversized ranch. He could envision the neighborhood when it was complete: young families, empty-nesters and everything in between. It would be warm and welcoming, and a place anyone would want to call home. He knew he sure as hell did. Living here would be perfect for him and for Max. Max, his six-year-old son, who was the amazing result from one monumental mistake.

He'd failed his son for the first few years of his life. He would do anything to make that up to him. He suspected that meant putting down roots in Cypress Corners, even if he wasn't sure how to do that.

Chapter 3

Noah knew Max was relying on his father to keep his head and prove that he could play with the big boys here in Cypress. Just last night, as Noah drove him back to his mother's place in Melbourne, he'd asked when he could stay with Noah for good. It had nearly killed Noah to say that couldn't happen right now.

His agreement with the boy's mother, a stripper he'd had a one-night stand with back in his beach bum days, only gave him weekend visitation. There was no such thing as custody in the state of Florida, but this was their parenting plan. She had Max the majority of the time, and Noah paid child support. And Nadine was a good mother to their son. She didn't dance any more, and was now working as a medical assistant.

He wanted Max for more than weekends, though. He'd been working so damn hard for the past few years he hadn't even been able to think about being a full-time dad. Up until last year Max had spent most of their weekends with Noah's mom and dad. That fact sat sour in his belly, and he was determined to settle into a permanent place and give Max more stability.

He wished that place could be Cypress Corners. Cypress had its own K-8 school right in the community, and whenever Noah saw the kids in their little khaki shorts and polos he pictured

Max walking right along with them. How awesome would it be to walk his son to school every morning? That was something even Nadine couldn't give him.

Noah reached the Sales Center and parked the golf cart at the curb. He couldn't rouse any enthusiasm for driving back to his apartment. He'd been living in St. Cloud for the past few months, a rural city a few miles west of Cypress. His apartment lacked any kind of architectural interest or warmth, and the best thing he could say about it was that when Max stayed over on the weekends he had his own room. During the week, though? It was lonely as hell.

Ben had offered him what might be the first step in making Cypress his home. Ben and his wife Tammy had moved into the big Craftsman right before Thanksgiving, and Tammy's townhouse near the town center was sitting vacant. Ben had suggested that Noah could rent the place, and he was seriously considering it.

Most days he put off driving back to St. Cloud for as long as possible. He'd stay out at one of the model homes long after closing and work on his tablet. Maybe he'd meet Ben or Ty Walsh for a beer over in the Town Tavern. Sometimes he'd even head out to the far lakeshore to just stare at the still water. In fact, he'd toyed with the idea of moving into the tent-cabin once Ty and Cassie had moved out, but there was only one room and no separate space for Max.

The kid loved the wild parts of Cypress, though. Maybe next weekend he'd arrange a tour of the east side of the property. He could think of a certain pretty woman who might be able help him out there.

He looked toward the parking lot and his silver truck, and made a decision. He'd hang out in Cypress for a while longer. It was only six o'clock. Yeah, twilight was coming but it wasn't like he was afraid of the dark.

After stopping at the town market for a six pack, he hopped back into the cart and made his way toward the far lakeshore. The path was a little bumpy, but the nubby tires made easy work of the sandy path. Darkness grew before he reached the turn off for the tent-cabin, but in Florida it wasn't unusual for sunset to tease and tempt with all of its colors for a long while before the sun slid under the horizon between breaths.

He found the place dark. Quiet, except for the frogs he could hear croaking just beyond in the reeds by the lakeshore. Parking the golf cart beside the thick trunk of a huge live oak tree, he got out and made his way to the back porch. A light popped on as he stepped up, but the glow wasn't harsh.

Settling into one of the Adirondack chairs, he cracked open a beer and gazed out over the rippling lake. The stars had just started to come out, and he felt a peace he hadn't experienced since leaving the surf behind.

He took a long sip of his beer, letting his mind work. He had to make a move. He knew that. For years now he'd felt like he was still floating, sitting on his board and waiting for a wave to come. What the hell was he waiting for now?

He could live here in Cypress. He could have an awesome place to take Max every weekend. Maybe he'd even be able to change his parenting plan and get to see his son more.

Ben wouldn't wait forever for his answer. Rental properties in Cypress were in high demand, given the great schools and amenities. He'd be an idiot to pass up the opportunity his friend offered. Did Noah want to live where he worked, though? That was the sticking point for him.

He wasn't sure about spending his nights so close to where he spent his days. He sucked in a breath and slowly let it out. The sounds of lapping water and rustling leaves had his heartrate slowing. The adrenaline rush he'd felt earlier had subsided, leaving him relaxed. Yeah. He could get used to living like this.

He lifted the bottle to his lips again.

"What are you doing out here?"

He nearly choked on his beer, sputtering as he turned his head to find Jessie standing beside the porch. She had her hands braced on her hips and that ugly sweater on again.

"Hey, Jessie." He saw sparks flashing in her eyes. "What are you doing here?"

"I live here."

His mind worked for a second. That explained the sparks. He shrugged. "Sorry, I didn't know. How long?"

She blinked at him. "What? Oh, I moved in last week. Why are you here?"

"Just came out to take in the view." He grabbed another beer and held it toward her. "Join me?"

Her gaze went from the bottle in his hand to his face, and he wondered what she was looking for. She must have seen something that put her at ease, because her shoulders relaxed a little.

"Okay." He opened her bottle and she took it from him, settling into the other chair. "So, why are you out here?"

"Told you." He took another drink of his beer. "Just came out for the view."

She took a sip and let out a breath. "Well, it's my view now."

"Lucky you." He meant it, too. She was a lucky girl to have this in her backyard. "I'm thinking of moving here, too."

It was her turn to choke. "W-where?"

He smiled. "Not right here, Jessie. To Cypress."

"Oh. Where do you live now?"

"St. Cloud."

"Hmm." She nodded. "I don't miss it."

"You lived there?"

"Yes."

It felt like there was something she wasn't saying, but who was he to press her?

"I sometimes hang around Cypress after work," he admitted. "There's nothing dragging me back to my apartment."

That truth was tough to admit. Except for Max, he had no one in his life worth driving ten minutes for. She didn't appear to think anything of it, though. In fact, she looked more relaxed than he'd ever seen her.

"I don't blame you for coming out here," she said, easing back in her chair. "I could look at this lake forever."

He looked at her instead. Her sweater had slipped open and

her lush little body was lit by the moon hanging out over the lake and the spotlight. Dragging his eyes from her rack, he finished his beer.

"So how did your tour go?" he asked.

"The one in the afternoon?" At his nod, she beamed a smile at him. "Great! They loved the whole thing, Noah. They got it, you know?"

"That's because of you."

Her mouth dropped open. "What?"

"You, Jessie. When you talk about Cypress and what it can mean? You light up like a firefly."

She snorted a little, covering her mouth with one hand. "Firefly? Hmm. I don't know if that's any better than Pixie, but I'll take it."

"Pixie?" He laughed softly. "Yeah, I can see that."

The lighting was dim on the porch but he caught the blush on her cheeks. "Never mind."

They both fell silent but he was very aware of the sound of her breathing. Of her scent, too. Those wildflowers were stronger out here in the still air. In the growing dark.

"How's the house coming?" she finally asked.

He couldn't help but grin. "It's going to be amazing. It's a huge one-story."

"I know," she said with a quirk of her full lips.

He chuckled. Of course she knew.

"Right," he said. "The slab's getting poured later this week."

She tilted her head to one side, studying him again. "You're excited."

"Oh I'm pumped, Jessie. No joke, this is going to be fantastic. It's all due to Ben's design, of course."

"And your implementation, Noah. You're the one who creates something from drawings and specs."

"Thanks." Pride warmed him inside and out. "Not everybody gets that."

Her brow puckered for a second. "I would love to be able to build something real."

Did she really not get just what she brought to the table? Why the big guys at Cypress spoke so highly of her?

"You do better than that, Jessie." He put his bottle down on the decking and reached over to cover her hand. It felt small and soft beneath his. "You create the *dream* of something for everybody you tour."

She gazed at him with what he could only call a hope to believe his words. Her eyes were wide and her lush lips were parted, and she appeared sweetly doubtful of her own gifts. He couldn't help it. He leaned in, breathed in her scent, and pressed his mouth to hers.

***

Jessie was stunned at the touch of Noah's kiss. He'd been looking at her with such warmth, such admiration, she'd been tempted to believe him. Heck, she'd melted. Now she could only feel heat and passion, and he tasted delicious. A little spicy and, mixed with the beer he'd been drinking, intoxicating. Leaning into him, she kissed him back.

He moaned softly in the back of his throat, the sound scraping over her skin to reach inside of her. She trembled, unable to keep from opening her mouth as he deepened the kiss. His tongue was strong. Agile in her mouth. Her pulse raced and she gripped onto his thick biceps in an effort to ground herself.

He placed both of his big hands on her waist, sliding them down just a bit to grab onto her hips. His touch was hot through her skirt, and made her shiver. She wanted to get closer to him. She wanted to crawl inside of him if she could, but the darn armrest of her chair kept her stuck in her seat.

She must have made a sound, of need or frustration she wasn't sure, because he pulled away from her.

His blue eyes were dark as he stared into hers. His pupils were huge and his nostrils flared. He looked really turned-on, and that made her breath come fast.

"I'm sorry," he rasped, moving one of those magic hands of his to cup her face. He had callouses on his wide palm and long fingers. Actual callouses from working with his hands. "I just had to kiss you."

She licked her lips, and saw that he watched her tongue. A flutter of heat spread through her body, then a wave of apprehension. She knew what came with kisses like that. What happened when she forgot to think and just felt. Surrender. Complete and utter surrender of everything that made her…her.

"That can't happen again," she whispered, her own words tight and breathy.

His well-sculpted mouth turned down a little. "If you say so." His blue eyes sparkled at her as he smiled again. "Although I gotta tell you, Jessie. You kiss like you do everything."

She couldn't help but think about the kiss they'd shared. It had been so perfect, until it wasn't.

"What does that mean?" she had to know.

A crooked smile lifted those delicious lips of his. "With all of you."

She didn't know what to say to that, and he spared her the trouble. After draining his bottle, he set it back in the cardboard six pack.

"I better take off." He rubbed his hands over his very fit thighs and stood. "I'll leave you to your lakeshore."

They looked at each other for a long minute, then she nodded.

"Thanks for the beer." She put her half-empty bottle on the deck and stood too, fingering the bottom button of her cardigan. "This was nice, Noah. Sitting and talking with you."

He dipped his head, looking at her from beneath his brows. "*Just* sitting and talking?"

And kissing. She couldn't talk about that, though. Not when she could still taste him on her tongue. Could still feel his hands on her body.

After another long minute, he grabbed up the six pack. "Good night, Jessie."

"Good night."

She watched him as he walked away, out of the light above the porch to be swallowed by the growing darkness, until she heard him start the near-silent motor of his golf cart. Lifting her bottle, she sank back into her chair.

45

It had been unexpected, seeing someone in what she now thought of as her place. It sure was different from when she'd found Shannon and Billy here, though.

Noah took up a lot of her place too, with those broad shoulders and long legs. He'd looked really nice sitting there, though. Comfortable. Like he belonged. With her, of all people.

Drawing on her beer, she let out a breath. She'd stopped at the tavern for pizza with Oliver before driving out here, and he'd teased her about her tour of Noah's houses. Something about hammers and nails, and maybe even screws. She'd blocked him out for the most part. Laughed off his not-so-subtle innuendo. He was so naughty sometimes.

Oliver was a doll man, though. And if he didn't play for the other team she might have had a crush on him when she'd started working here, along with all the other hot guys in Cypress. Now she counted him as a good friend, in spite of his teasing about Noah. She didn't want to imagine what would happen if he ever found out she'd sat out at her lakeshore with the man. Or, horrors, that she'd kissed him? Yikes.

She'd loved that kiss, though. It was soft and sweet. Hard and hot. Deep and delicious. She knew she would dream about that kiss. Heck, she *had* dreamed about it, if she were being honest with herself. She'd been right to tell him it couldn't happen again.

For nearly five years now she'd avoided any kind of sexual contact. Any kind of physical contact at all, really. It didn't matter how perfect Noah's mouth had felt on hers. It didn't matter how much she'd wanted him to use those big, capable hands of his on her body, either. She couldn't bring herself to risk everything again. To give everything to another person and have it ruined. Twisted into something hateful. And painful.

She finished her beer and wished for another for just a second. Only for a second. She wasn't Shannon, after all. Free with alcohol and free with her body. Shannon did tend to fall hard for a few of her one-nighters, though. Jessie had nursed her through hangovers of the body, and of the heart, on too many occasions to count. A pang of guilt struck her.

She told herself that Shannon was a big girl now. That she could look after herself. That Jessie wasn't her keeper any longer. It was a tough habit to break.

She wrapped her sweater around herself again and let out a breath. She had enough on her plate to worry about her sister now. Her work at the Sales Center. Her work at the Institute. Settling into her new home. Noah.

Noah wasn't really a concern though, was he? He wasn't hers to worry over or to dream about, for that matter. He was hot and smart and capable. She imagined he could handle himself just fine. But oh, the memory of how he'd looked leaning easily against the column of that model home made her tingle right now. And surrounded by his spicy hot scent as they'd talked in the peace and quiet out here. She'd watched his mouth as he'd talked. As he'd drunk his beer. She'd kissed that full, delicious mouth. She'd reached out and grabbed on to those strong arms, holding tight as she lost herself.

No. She rubbed a hand over her face. She couldn't lose herself. She wouldn't lose herself. Not again.

And if that meant staying away from Noah and every temptation he posed, that was just her too bad.

Chapter 4

Noah sat nursing his cup of coffee in the break room at the Sales Center on Wednesday morning. He knew it was safe to be there today. So maybe he was being a coward. He could live with that. Jessie was at the Cypress Institute and he didn't have to worry about running into her.

Not that he didn't want to catch of glimpse of her. He didn't want to risk seeing the fear in her eyes that he'd seen Monday night, though. Man, that kiss had been amazing before she'd pulled away. She'd tasted so fresh and hot, and when she'd grabbed on to him he'd wanted to drag her down to the wood planking on the deck and taste all of her. Then she'd stiffened, and he couldn't do anything but leave her alone. He had to keep leaving her alone, too. There was something there and he had no clue how to figure her out.

"Hey, man," Ben Chapman said as he joined him. "You don't usually hang around here in the morning."

"Stem walls and rebar are just about set," Noah said. "The rough plumb is happening this afternoon."

The stem walls, reinforced with steel bars, would not only assure that Ben's design would be more energy efficient. The home would be more secure in Florida's changeable climate.

Hurricane-force winds wouldn't be a match for the large home. That was the intention, anyway.

Ben nodded. "Yeah, I saw the schedule. Thanks for keeping me updated."

Noah lifted his cup in salute. Ben continued to watch him, though, his eyes narrowed.

Noah set his cup back down on the table. "What?"

"That still doesn't explain why you're here," Ben said. "On the last three models, you've personally supervised the plumbers."

"Maybe I trust them?"

Ben chuckled. "Yeah, I trust you but I still check on your every step when one of my designs is being built."

Noah barked out a laugh. "That's why I love working with you, man. You're even more anal than I am."

Ben grinned. "So…why aren't you out there?"

"I'm heading out there soon. I just wanted to veg for a couple of minutes."

"Noah." Ben crossed his arms as he leaned back in his chair. "You don't 'veg.' Not in all the time I've known you. I've never seen you 'chill,' either. Why today?"

Noah shrugged. It wasn't long before realization dawned on

Ben's face. His eyes rounded and his mouth gaped. Noah dropped his gaze to the tabletop. *Shit.*

"Oh, I get it," Ben said. "Today's Wednesday. You're here because she isn't."

Noah stared at him, striving to keep a blank look on his face. "I don't know who you're talking about."

Ben held up a hand. "Look, I know Jessie can be a little prickly. She's our connection to the Institute, though. Just ask her something, anything, about conservation or the environment and she'll open up. She'll get you the answers you need."

Noah gave a silent prayer of thanks that Ben hadn't guessed the real reason he was avoiding Jessie. He'd gotten her to open up for a few heart-stopping moments out there by the lakeshore. Even before they'd kissed, he'd learned that she doubted herself. That she so wanted to believe him when he told her how awesome she was at her job.

He also knew that if he saw her he'd have a hard time keeping himself from kissing her again.

"Yeah, I'll do that." He turned his cup on the table for a minute, and then decided to just ask. "So. Jessie. What's her story?"

Ben's brows arched. Every guy knew what that question

meant, and Noah knew that Ben was no exception. That question meant that Noah was interested.

"I have no idea." Ben leaned closer. "I could ask Tammy."

Noah pulled back, his lungs seizing. "No, man. That's okay."

"They're pretty close," Ben went on.

"That's the problem. Women tell each other everything."

"Are you worried about Jessie telling my wife something, Noah?"

"No." He drew out the word, and immediately regretted it.

They were both quiet for a beat.

"Is there something to tell?" Ben finally asked.

Noah began to shake his head when Oliver breezed into the break room.

"Something to tell about what?" he asked.

Noah and Ben both started mumbling something or other, but Oliver wasn't fooled.

He smirked, and then settled down at their table. "Is this gossip? Ooh, does one of you have a deep, dark secret?" He frowned at Ben. "Ben, tell me you're not keeping something from my bestie Tammy."

"Hey, we're just talking," Ben said.

"Nothing to tell," Noah added.

Oliver slanted them both a look, then threw up his hands. "Straight guys. You just don't seem to grasp the concept of juicy gossip."

Noah crossed his arms to mimic Ben's posture, keeping his expression even. "No gossip, Oliver. Nothing to tell," he said again for good measure.

"What are you three roosters crowing about?" Tammy asked as she joined them.

Noah came quickly to his feet. He wasn't going to say anything about Jessie in front of Ben's wife.

"I'm off to the work site," he said.

Oliver eyed him, his lips pursed. "Our newest rooster is sitting on some eggs." He laughed at himself. "Or something."

"Or nothing, Oliver." Noah nodded to Tammy and turned. "Gotta go. See you later."

"See you, man," Ben said.

Noah made it three whole steps out of the room before conversation exploded behind him. That was just great. He knew his buddy Ben pretty well, though. He wouldn't talk about Noah and Jessie, even if he suspected something. He might say something just to Tammy, but not in front of Oliver.

He stepped outside and threw a glance toward the Cypress Institute. He wasn't sure what Jessie did over there every Wednesday, but he sure as hell wasn't going to find out today. Instead, he got into his now-favorite golf cart and headed out to the site.

He'd think about Jessie later, though. He'd relive that kiss, too. And wonder just what it was she was afraid of.

She was a package wrapped a little too tight, and he itched for the chance to find out what was inside.

***

Jessie peered at the computer screen, clicking through Dr. Robbins' appointments for the afternoon. All were complete, she was pleased to note. It was just past four o'clock now, and there was little left for her to do here today.

Dr. Robbins, the director of the Cypress Institute, had suggested she come work one day a week here soon after she'd joined the Cypress sales team. Rick Chapman, her boss, and Mr. Forbes, the developer himself, had both encouraged the job share. They'd seen her interest and aptitude for all things green, and knew the connection would only serve to help sales. That connection was another thing that made living and working in Cypress Corners a dream come true.

"Hey there, Jessie," Harmony Chapman said as she entered the reception area through the front doors.

Jessie smiled at Rick's wife. "Hi, Harmony."

Harmony had obviously been riding her beloved electric scooter out over the property. Her skin looked sun-kissed and several of her honey-colored curls had escaped her ponytail. Jessie knew Harmony was just past thirty but she looked about Jessie's age this afternoon.

"What are you doing at Becky's desk?" Harmony asked.

Jessie took off her glasses and set them on the work station. "Becky had to go up to Orlando this afternoon, so I stepped in."

Harmony feigned an expression of surprise. "Dr. Robbins actually let you leave the lab?"

Jessie laughed. "For a couple of hours, yes."

The lab was Harmony's domain as Plant Conservationist, but on Wednesdays she preferred to do her field work. Harmony liked being outdoors more than indoors, as she'd told Jessie many times. Jessie was inclined to agree with her, except when it came to possible encounters with the wildlife that shared the property with the residents.

"I didn't have a chance to ask you," Harmony began. "How did you do on your first eco-tour?"

"I think it went really well," Jessie said. "The two couples were sweet, and clearly they already bought into the whole thing before they even climbed into the cart."

Harmony nodded. "Good, good. That's half the battle. What about the green neighborhood? How did the models look?"

Jessie swallowed as she thought about just how good the model homes had looked, especially the one that Noah had propped up with one of his broad shoulders. "They looked good."

Harmony tilted her head to one side. "Are you feeling okay? You're a little flushed."

Jessie wrapped her cardigan more tightly around her waist. "I feel fine."

"It must be the sweater then." Harmony waved toward the wide glass doors that looked out on the front walk of the Institute. "It's over eighty degrees today, Jessie. It's only going to get hotter."

"So?" Jessie gestured to the khaki shorts she wore when she worked at the Institute. "It's chilly in here with the A/C."

"Still, it's almost April. Maybe it's time to ditch the sweater?"

Jessie ran her hands across the nubby knit of the sweater she wore over her Cypress Institute polo. And her shorts, if she were being honest. The sweater was big.

She'd discovered it in a consignment shop more than five years ago. It was knit in varying shades of beige, and always reminded her of oatmeal. The buttons were thick horn, and just the size of her thumbnail. She knew it wasn't very pretty, but the sturdy garment was her go-to sweater/jacket/blanket.

"I don't wear it in the summer," she offered.

"I hope not," Harmony laughed.

Jessie smiled a little. "I guess I can let it go in a couple of weeks."

Harmony lifted a brow and Jessie's smile widened.

"Okay, okay," Jessie said, lifting her hands in defeat. "I'll rethink my sweater choice."

Harmony gave a sharp nod. "Good. You know, Claire wears the prettiest cardigans. Why don't you try something like that? You know. If you don't want to abandon the whole sweater thing completely."

Claire, Jake Chapman's wife and the CPA Controller for Cypress Corners, did have a lovely wardrobe. She liked sweaters too, but usually wore them in yummy colors like lemon yellow, mint green and her signature color, poppy orange.

"I guess," Jessie said. "She does wear such pretty clothes."

"And she's an expert at finding bargains, too."

Jessie brightened. "Oh, I should go up to the outlets in Orlando."

"Sure." Harmony ran her hands over her own worn and comfortable-looking camp shirt and khaki shorts. "Maybe I could use some clothes, too."

"Road trip?"

Harmony smiled. "Maybe. I'll get with Claire and let you know when we'll go up to Orlando. Cassie might want to come, too."

Jessie shook her head. "I doubt Cassie buys her stuff at the outlets, Harmony."

Harmony nodded. "Yeah, she brought a lot of stuff with her when she came down here about a year ago. Still, she loves to take Riley shopping. She'll take any excuse she can get."

"Cool," Jessie said. "Just keep me posted."

Harmony waved and headed down the corridor to check in with Dr. Robbins. Jessie didn't need to announce her. That was for sure.

Jessie stroked her arm, feeling the thick knit once again. Yeah, she could use some new clothes. At the very least she could get some new running stuff. And maybe some pretty clothes for work at the Sales Center. Maybe a new sweater, too. One in a gorgeous shade of blue she couldn't seem to get out of her head. The exact blue of Noah's eyes.

Shaking her head, she put him out of her mind. He kept sneaking in there, darn it. And that kiss? She was pretty sure she'd think about that for a while, too.

She smiled to herself as her mind turned to Ty and Cassie's little niece, Riley. They were a family, even though Riley spent a lot of time with her father in St. Cloud. Ty was like a father to the little girl, though. A lot like her father had been. Caring and funny and indulgent. Maybe her dad had been a little too indulgent.

She'd been stunned when he'd died of a brain aneurism. Adrift, she'd latched onto the first guy who showed her affection after that loss. Mitch had helped fill her loneliness. He'd been handsome and charming, and the perfect boyfriend. Until he wasn't. She fingered the spot high on her left cheekbone, feeling the echo of the pain she'd felt when he'd hit her. Wrapping her sweater around her once more, she shivered. Her chill had nothing to do with the air conditioning. It was the thought of giving every bit of herself to someone who took even more and mistreated her, too.

Pushing thoughts of Mitch out of her head was a lot easier than getting Noah to vacate the premises. She wasn't really afraid to think about Noah, though. He was even better looking than Mitch had been but, more importantly, she wasn't dependent on Noah for her emotional wellbeing. She also wasn't twenty-one anymore. It would be a long time before she trusted a guy like she'd trusted Mitch.

She brushed her bangs back from her head, a nervous gesture she fully acknowledged, and put her glasses back on. A glance at the time in the corner of the computer screen showed her that it was nearly five now. The Institute closed up shop in just about ten minutes and then she could head back out to the tent-cabin. Her sanctuary. Her home.

Again, Noah popped into her head. Noah had surprised her when she discovered him out on her back porch. And he'd thrilled her with the best kiss she'd ever tasted.

He seemed different from Mitch. He'd pulled back when she'd freaked out, for one thing. Now she just had to avoid having any contact with him. But oh, those eyes. That build. That smile.

She was even less sure of accomplishing that than she was

of keeping him out of her head.

Chapter 5

As Noah drove back from Melbourne Friday evening, he glanced in the rearview mirror and checked on Max for what felt like the fortieth time. They'd stopped by his parents' place for a visit, and the little boy's hair was still mussed from where his mother had "hugged the stuffing out of him," as she always said.

The kid was playing his tablet at the moment, which Nadine had decreed was allowed as long as he didn't play for more than thirty minutes. That would just about get them to Cypress Corners. The ride past Cypress into St. Cloud would make for a pretty long ten minutes. Once again, he wished he could just pull into Cypress and be home. He might not have a place there yet, but he could spend a little bit of time.

"Hey, buddy?" he asked.

"Yeah?" Max answered absently, his blond head still bent over the screen.

"Wanna eat at the Town Tavern?"

"What's that?" He lifted his head a little and met Noah's eyes in the rearview.

"A restaurant in Cypress Corners."

"Where you work?" Max's voice was raised in obvious interest.

"Yep." Noah had only brought him to Cypress a couple of times in the months he'd been working here, and a pang of guilt struck him. He pushed it aside and took his son's interest as the positive thing it was. "We can grab a couple of burgers or a pizza."

Max grinned. "Pizza!"

Noah chuckled. "Pizza it is."

The wide entrance of Cypress came up on the right side of the road, so he slowed the Ford F-150 and steered the truck into the property. The long main drive was bracketed by white ranch fencing and tall leafy trees, and led them toward the center of town. It was very different from the ranch and farm land they'd passed on the drive from the coast. The place was quaint and welcoming. Like a picture postcard of some small town where he'd love to raise Max.

"This place looks nice," Max said.

"It is nice." He slowed as they passed the coffee shop, and then pulled to a stop on the corner. "The Clubhouse is straight ahead. That's a little fancy for two guys eating pizza on a Friday night, though."

"Where are we eating?"

"Right next door." Noah found a space in the parking lot

and cranked off the engine. He opened the back door and leaned in to unbuckle Max's car seat. "Come on, buddy."

Max set his tablet on the seat and hopped up and out of the truck. "I'm starving!"

Noah smiled, ruffling Max's corn silk hair. "Good. How about sausage?"

"Sounds good, Daddy."

Noah steered him toward the entrance to the Town Tavern and pulled open the heavy wooden door. They stepped into the waiting area and Noah watched Max take in every detail. The tavern was done like an English pub, with dark woods and green-shaded lights and a lot of brass. The place looked crowded too, which was to be expected on a Friday.

"Two for dinner, please," he told the girl working the hostess stand. "Name's Brady."

She smiled. "We'll call you when your table's ready."

"Noah!" Ben called from the takeout counter just off the waiting area.

Noah raised a hand in greeting as he and Max made their way over. "Hey, Ben."

Ben nodded to him and then eyed Max. "How you doing, Max?"

Ben was the one person Max had met when Noah brought him out to the job site over the holidays.

"Good," Max said.

"I'm picking up takeout," Ben said. "Tammy wants a big, juicy burger. She's growing a carnivore, apparently."

Noah smiled. "We're just stopping by for some pizza."

"On your way to St. Cloud?" Ben asked. When Noah nodded, Ben shook his head. "You know, you could change that. Driving all the way to St. Cloud every night."

"What's he mean, Daddy?" Max piped up.

Noah looked down at his son, thinking about the offer Ben had made more than once. Tammy's townhouse was just a couple of streets from the town center, and would be pretty perfect. If he decided to go for it.

"I might be able to get a place here," he told Max.

Max's eyes went round. "Really?"

"Do you like Cypress Corners, Max?" Ben asked him.

"I guess," the little boy answered. "Daddy builds houses here."

"Houses that Ben designs," Noah said.

Max just nodded at that bit of information.

"You haven't spent much time here, huh Max?" Ben asked.

Max shook his head.

"We've been sticking to St. Cloud and Kissimmee on the weekends," Noah said.

"Oh, yeah?" Ben asked. "Been out to Old Town Village?"

Max's face lit up. "Yeah! We love that place, don't we Daddy?"

Noah smiled and placed his hand on the top of Max's head. "We do, buddy. Lots of fun out there."

"My sister Cassie and her husband Ty take Riley out there all the time," Ben told Max.

"Riley?" Max asked.

"Ty's niece," Noah said. "She's about four now, I think."

"Riley's a girl?" Max asked, wrinkling his nose.

"Afraid so, pal," Ben said. "You should meet my nephew Nick. He's about your age. What are you, five?"

Max puffed out his chest. "Six."

Ben slowly nodded, a look of respect stamped on his face. "My mistake." He looked at Noah again. "Why don't you bring Max by Rick and Harmony's on Sunday? Around one o'clock."

"The barbeque?" Noah guessed.

Ben grinned. "You know it. My big brother loves to cook meat over fire."

Noah thought for a second. Rick had extended an open invitation to the barbeque picnic he and Harmony had nearly every Sunday. Another thing that set Cypress apart from other developments in Florida, the Sales Center was closed on the weekends. Forbes, and by extension Rick, wanted family to be first and foremost in the community. Having mothers and fathers work on the weekend wasn't the way to do that.

Noah hadn't made the time to go to one of the picnics since he'd been at Cypress. He and Max usually rolled around St. Cloud or Kissimmee all weekend and then he had to get the boy back to Nadine's Sunday evening. She was reasonable, though. She never gave him a deadline or anything.

He looked down at Max. "What do you think, buddy? Do you want to go to a picnic on Sunday before we head back to your mom's?"

Max nodded, a big smile splitting his face. "Yes, yes, yes!"

Noah laughed and looked at Ben. "Tell Rick we'll try to make it." He winked at his son. "I think Max really wants to meet Nick."

Ben nodded. "Will do." The kid working the takeout counter brought over two bags of food and Ben stood. "I'll see you guys Sunday, then."

"See you, man," Noah said.

"Brady," the girl called from the waiting area. "Your table's ready."

Noah placed a hand on Max's shoulder and the two of them followed the hostess to their table. They ordered their drinks, soda for Noah and a lemonade for Max, and sat there. Noah could tell Max was thinking about everything Ben had said. He was fiddling with the edge of his napkin, nibbling on his lower lip.

"What do you think, Max?" Noah began.

Max's head shot up. "About the pizza?"

"No, buddy. About getting a place here."

Noah caught the glimmer in his blue eyes. The kid favored his mother with his light blond hair and finely-boned face, but his eyes were all Noah. He was a looker. That was for sure.

"Maybe we can hang around here for a little while before the picnic on Sunday," Noah said. "Sounds good?"

Max grinned. "Sounds good."

Noah shoved aside his uncertainty and chose to focus on the very real possibility of putting down roots in a place where he worked. Where his friends were. Where he was certain to run into Jessie.

And suddenly, it felt like a really good idea.

***

Jessie parked her Jeep at the curb in front of Harmony and Rick's gorgeous home. It was situated in one of the more exclusive villages of Cypress, and commanded a great view of the main lakeshore across the street. It was set on a large lot, and was painted a dove gray with a peaked slate roof. A deep porch stretched across the front of the house, dotted with Adirondack chairs and a hanging bench swing. Columns and a railing enclosed the porch, making it look very inviting.

She knew the features of the homes in Cypress, both cosmetic and technological, and she knew her boss's wouldn't disappoint. The homes in Cypress, whether in the higher-end villages like this one or in the more densely-populated ones, were state-of-the-art. Though traditional in design and appearance, they were at their guts wired for the homeowners' every convenience. And now that they were building a village with a heavy leaning toward the environment? She suspected she could look forward to a very successful career here.

Climbing up the wide steps to the front porch, she shifted the spring-green cardboard box of pastries she'd picked up at the bakery in the town center. She couldn't begin to make anything like Claire Chapman did and, besides, where would she bake in the tent-cabin? A quick rap on the wooden screen door brought the sweet little face of Harmony and Rick's five-year-old son, Nick.

"Hey, Jessie!" He pushed open the door, holding onto the handle. "I have a new friend."

She blinked at the little boy's disclosure. "Oh, that's nice."

When he ran back into the house, she could hear voices coming from the interior. She took a second to look over her outfit. She'd gone up to the outlet center with Claire and Harmony on Saturday morning, and found a few things to spruce up her wardrobe. Everything had to be wash and wear, since she wasn't going to start ironing clothes out in the tent-cabin and she sure as heck wasn't going to haul her clothes to the drycleaner's.

So today she wore a crisp pair of tan linen shorts and a buttoned sleeveless top in a yummy shade of lemon. She did wear a sweater, but this new one was a thin white knit and crossed with narrow horizontal lines of cotton candy pink and the same yellow as her top. She felt light and springy, right down to her new pink leather ballet flats.

Stepping through the open screen door, she looked around the marble-tiled entry. "Hello?"

"Jessie!" Harmony came from the direction of the kitchen and gave her a warm hug before pulling her back into the main part of the house. "I'm so glad you came."

"Thanks for having me," Jessie said, holding out the bakery box. "I brought these."

"Ooh, thank you. I love the bakery, but don't tell Claire I sweet cheat on her."

Jessie laughed. "I won't. I'm sure she brought something phenomenal today."

"She did." Harmony led her to the kitchen and waved at a clear plastic container. "Chocolate-chocolate chip. Oh, she has my number."

Jessie nodded and looked around. She'd been here many times before, but she could never get over how Harmony had made the gorgeous oversized interior into a cozy home. The great room had a floor to ceiling stacked-stone fireplace and was completely open to the kitchen. Light granite, tons of cabinets and a tall counter with barstools made this space perfect for the ever-growing Chapman family.

Harmony looked Jessie over, head to toe. "I love those clothes on you."

"Me, too," Claire Chapman said as she stepped in through

the French doors that led to the patio. "You look so sweet."

Jessie didn't mind the description. She'd been called that for so long it was just a part of her.

"Thanks, Claire. I think I could develop a serious habit of shopping with you."

Claire beamed. "Hey, you gotta know what you're after when you go hunting."

"That's an interesting way to put it," Jessie said.

Claire tucked a thick strand of strawberry blond hair behind one ear. "I can teach you much, grasshopper."

Jessie laughed. "I don't know if I'm ready."

"Oh, you are," Harmony said, pouring her a tall glass of lemonade. "You are so ready."

Jessie held up her hands. "Okay, okay. I left the oatmeal sweater at home today, didn't I?"

Claire and Harmony shared a look and then both grinned.

"It does look like oatmeal," Harmony said with a laugh.

"Never mind," Jessie said. "So Nick told me he has a new friend?"

Harmony brightened. "Yes! Noah brought Max with him."

Jessie's stomach flipped over. Her cheeks flamed. "Noah's here?"

"What's with the blush?" Claire asked. Then her eyes went wide. "Oh, you like Noah!"

"Shh." Jessie looked around, relieved to her soul that there didn't appear to be anyone else in earshot at the moment. "Jeez what are we, in middle school?"

Claire clicked her tongue. "All right. But I should warn you about these Chapman picnics."

Jessie glanced at Harmony, who kept her face suspiciously blank. "What is it about these Chapman picnics, exactly?"

"They're notorious for getting sparks going," Claire said.

"Sparks?" Yeah, she'd experienced those first hand by the lake with Noah that night. "Oh, I'm not worried about any sparks."

"Okay," Harmony said. "But those sparks are inevitably seen later by dear Lettie Fairfax, Jessie."

Jessie gaped at her friends. "Oh, that woman always seems to be talking about something naughty even when she's talking about the weather."

Claire laughed. "Doesn't she just?"

Jessie grabbed her glass of lemonade and took a long drink. That seemed to give her a few seconds to collect herself before she blushed even redder. Noah was here. Sparks.

Then she heard it. The laughter of children drifting in through the French doors. Children, not just one child.

"Harmony," Jessie began. "Who's Max?"

Harmony looked at her for a beat. "Jessie, Max is Noah's son."

Jessie could only stare back at her. *His son?*

Chapter 6

Noah nursed his bottle of beer, watching Max play on the lawn with Rick and Harmony's son Nick. The easy banter between Rick and his brother Jake felt comfortable to him as they rehashed old stories and gave each other the business, and Noah knew he didn't have to contribute anything. Ben and his wife sat on the other side of the picnic table, in a quiet conversation. Noah had never had any of this. Not siblings to share a beer with and not a woman to share a life with.

He'd breezed through his life, happily taking whatever came easiest to him. Catching a wave or getting laid was never tough for him. Put the board in the water and float until the ocean brought a thrill. Smile and flirt with the hot girl until she dropped her panties. Hell, he hadn't even tried to have a kid and he was blessed with the best one he could imagine.

Max's big grin told him he'd found a buddy here, and Nick seemed just as happy to play with Max.

"They're too cute, those boys," Tammy said, leaning her arms on the table. "Before you know it, they'll be going to school together." She winked. "And getting into trouble together."

Noah gave a shake of his head. "Max lives in Melbourne."

"For now," Ben said. "So, how about it?"

Noah couldn't think of a reason to turn down Ben's offer again. In fact, since Friday night he'd been imagining just how great it would be to bring Max home to Cypress every weekend. Hell, more than the weekend if he and Nadine could work something out.

"I'd be a fool to pass this up," he admitted to Ben. He took a breath. "I'll take it."

Tammy clasped her hands. "You're renting the townhouse? That's great, Noah."

Noah smiled. "I really appreciate the offer. Just text me the particulars?"

Tammy nodded, her eyes bright. "Yes, we'll—" Her gaze shifted to the patio doors. "You came!"

He turned his head to see Jessie framed in the doorway. She looked so pretty standing there, even with an expression of uncertainty on her face and a glass of lemonade held in her hands. His mind flashed back to those heated minutes out by the lake. She'd gripped him just as tightly with those hands, her touch just right. He forced himself to set the memory aside.

She'd said that can't happen again. He wasn't exactly sure why not, he knew he sure as hell wanted that and more, but he sensed the Pixie was a lot stronger than she looked. She'd stick by her convictions, damn it all.

Her clothes today were brighter and seemed like they were more her size, and the effect was sweetly sexy. That kind of summed her up, really. Sweet and sexy.

"Hi, Tammy," she said with a small wave of one hand.

She stepped out onto the patio and glided over to the picnic table, her eyes on him. She didn't wear her glasses and he could see every shade of gold in those big amber eyes.

"Hey, Jessie," he said.

Her face was a little flushed but the color looked good on her. "Hey, Noah."

They stared at each other for a minute, and he was suddenly aware of a lull in the conversations that had been going on at the table. A flick of his eyes showed Ben and Tammy watching them closely, and he saw that even Jake was also looking on with an amused smile tilting his mouth.

"How do you want your burger, Jessie?" Rick asked from his position at the massive gas grill.

Jessie started a little, and then smiled at their host. "Just this side of pink."

"A woman after my own heart," Noah put in.

Her mouth opened just a bit, and then she recovered by biting her full lower lip. He couldn't help but stare.

Thankfully, Ben stood and joined his brother at the grill. Soon a platter of big, juicy burgers sat in the middle of the table and everyone began to eat. Claire and Harmony stepped out of the house, their heads together. When they both looked at him, the hairs on the back of his neck rose. What the hell was going on?

"Come on, Nick," Rick called. "Max, you too."

The boys tumbled together as they ran toward the patio.

"Uh, wash those hands," Harmony said.

The boys hurried past the adults into the house and Noah couldn't help but smile. It was so nice to see Max with a kid around his own age. Noah never got the chance to see him play outside much, and never with another kid.

"So you're taking Tammy's townhouse?" Rick asked him.

Noah nodded. "Yes. It'll be great not having to drive into St. Cloud every night."

"And Max will be able to spend more time with Nick," Harmony added.

Jessie's eyes were intent on him. "Max lives with you in St. Cloud?"

Noah met her gaze. "No. He lives with his mother in Melbourne."

He wanted to tell her more. For some reason he wanted to make it clear that he didn't have a relationship with Max's mother. But then the boys came out and settled at the table, nudging each other with their shoulders as they each took a fat hotdog.

Noah lifted the ketchup bottle and squeezed it onto Max's dog. "Nick?"

Nick nodded and Noah dressed his lunch, too.

"I'll never get why kids like ketchup instead of mustard on their hotdogs," Ben observed.

Tammy laughed. "Our little ravioli will probably like marinara sauce."

Ben gave her a look of mock-fear. "Horrifying."

Noah smiled and dug into the best burger he'd ever eaten. He saw that Jessie ate delicately but she looked as pleased with her lunch as Noah was.

By the time the boys were finished and back on the lawn, Noah managed to catch Jessie's gaze.

"How are you, Jessie?"

She flashed a bright smile. "Great, thanks."

"That's good."

"I didn't know you'd be here, you know," she said.

"Don't worry. I didn't think you were stalking me."

He'd tried for humor but for some reason she didn't smile.

"I would never do that," she said in a small voice.

Whoa. "I'm teasing, Jessie."

The smile she gave him wasn't as bright as the other. "Right." She swallowed. "I know."

He felt a flicker of something. He'd seen her shy. He'd seen her busy. He'd seen her completely engaged. He'd never seen her afraid. And unless he missed his guess, she wasn't about to tell him just what she feared. Why the hell would she? He was just a guy she'd known for a few months. One who worked where she did, and managed to kiss her senseless beside her little slice of heaven on the far lakeshore.

"Max," he called, coming to his feet.

"Yeah, Daddy?" Max said, lifting his head.

Noah smiled to see how mussed up the little boy looked. Dirt smudged and hair standing on end, he looked like he'd had a blast today. Once again, the decision to take Tammy's townhouse felt so right.

"Time to head out, buddy."

Max and Nick both groaned. Max walked slowly toward the patio, kicking at the grass. "Okay," he said, drawing out the last syllable.

"Go hit the bathroom, then. We have a long ride." After Max went back into the house, Noah turned to Rick and Harmony. "Thanks for inviting us."

"Anytime," Rick said.

"It's an open invitation, Noah." Harmony smiled at Max. "You and Max are always welcome."

Warmth spread through him at her words. "Thanks."

He could feel Jessie watching him, so he made sure to only glance at her before saying his goodbyes to everyone else.

"That was great, Daddy," Max said as they walked outside to Noah's truck.

"I'm glad, buddy." He got him into the back and buckled him in. "Max, what do you think about staying here with me on the weekends? You know, in Cypress Corners?"

Max's little face lit up. "I'd love it! I could play with Nick any time I wanted."

"That's true." He couldn't resist, so he dropped a kiss on top of Max's head. "Maybe by next weekend we'll be out of the apartment and right here."

Max smiled, and then yawned. "Sounds good."

Noah started the truck and steered them out of Cypress and toward Melbourne. For a second he was pulled back, like he wasn't meant to leave. He'd never managed to plant roots in the sand out in Melbourne. He could feel them growing into the lush landscape of Cypress today.

He wasn't sure how he felt about that.

***

Jessie slid on her rubber boots and headed out to take a shower. The tent-cabin boasted an outdoor bathroom, but it was completely plumbed with both hot and cold water. This part of the lakeshore was set to be developed in the coming years, but with the boon in single-family and a planned fifty-five plus community to the south of her place, her slice of waterfront was safe for now. It didn't take much imagination, especially for someone in sales, to see the potential for this section of the property. Infrastructure was far from complete, but she knew that if more people wanted what she had right now? It wouldn't take much to connect those structures to utilities as well.

She hummed to herself as she showered and shampooed. Her bathroom might be outside but she didn't have to share it with Shannon. That alone was worth the boots-and-flashlight nighttime visits.

She dried off and clomped back inside, so ready to change into a comfy top and pajama pants. Her hair was practically dry just from using her thick towel, a perk of having short hair. She pulled on a thin long-sleeve top in spring green and paired it with her Tinkerbell bottoms. It might be a little on the nose, but she liked the little Pixie. Maybe that was why she really didn't mind her Cypress nickname.

There was a bottle of white wine chilling in her little fridge, so she poured herself a glass and went out onto her back deck. Taking in a deep breath, she let go of the confusion of the day with the exhale. It was twilight now, and she should be relaxed. She'd spent a lovely day with friends. She got to look her fill at the guy who'd filled her thoughts since Monday night. And his son. She couldn't get over that revelation.

The boy was adorable, though. And seemed like a sweetheart, from the way he'd quickly bonded with Nick Chapman. Max lived with his mother, Noah had said. What was Noah's relationship with his ex like?

"Doesn't matter, does it?" she asked herself softly.

She took a sip of her wine and gazed out at her lakeshore. The night was coming on, but she could still see glints of the waning sunlight on the ripples over the water. It was nearly this time on Monday when she'd discovered Noah here. She glanced at the empty chair next to her. He'd sat right beside her in that chair. Closing her eyes, she relived that amazing kiss. She'd trembled. Her heart had raced. And then skidded to a stop.

A sound reached her and her eyes popped open. An engine, she guessed. Of a good-sized pickup truck. She had a sinking suspicion about just whose truck that was. With a sense of inevitability, she set her glass down and went inside to pour another one for her guest.

The truck door slammed and big booted footsteps sounded on the front porch. The wooden door rattled a little as he knocked on it, and she padded over the rag rug to open it. Gazing up, she drank in the view. He still wore the worn light blue polo shirt and cargo shorts that hung off his narrow hips. His clothes sure fit him just right, casual though they were. Well, wasn't she in her pajamas?

"Hey, Noah," she said for the second time today.

He dipped his head a little, looking at her from beneath his lashes. "Hey, Jessie."

She stepped back and he walked in, easily filling her small living space. Handing him the wineglass, she watched as he

84

arched a brow.

"This is mine?" he asked, taking it.

"Yep. Mine's out here." She turned from him and walked out to the back deck.

She settled back into her chair as he joined her.

"You knew I was coming?" he asked with a crooked smile.

"No." She waited for him to sit in what she was trying hard not to think of as *his chair*. "It's hard to miss the sound of your truck, though."

He took a sip of wine and shrugged. "I was driving back from Melbourne and found myself pulling into Cypress again."

"Instead of St. Cloud." It wasn't a question. "Why here, then?" That was a question, and one she wasn't going to wait to ask.

"I'm not sure."

The fading sunlight caught the blue of his eyes. Turning from the tempting picture he made, all long legs, broad shoulders and compelling gaze, she forced her eyes to the lake.

They sat for a few minutes, drinking their wine and sharing the view. It was more comfortable and quiet than she could have imagined, considering that he was such a big guy.

"Max is adorable," she said after a while.

"He's a good kid," he said. "I wish I had him for more than the weekends."

Jessie nodded. "That must suck."

He chuckled at her words. "It does."

She shook her head. "I mean, for him. I miss my father every day."

Out of the corner of her eye she saw him turned to her. "You lost your father?"

She nodded, her throat thick. "Five years ago."

His eyes grew cloudy. "I'm sorry."

As far as responses went, that was a pretty common one. Coming from Noah, though? It felt genuine. It must be those eyes of his. Sincerity, tenderness and heat. How did he manage that expression?

"Thanks."

"What about your mom?"

She gave a quick shake of her head. "She's been gone since I was little." She drank more of her wine and faced him again. "What about your parents?"

He threw her a smile. "Alive and well, I'm happy to say. They live out in Melbourne, too."

"Did you grow up there?"

"Born practically on the beach," he said with a grin. "I miss the ocean, but your lake is a nice substitute."

"My lake." She let out a breath. "It does really feel like my lake now."

"In just a couple of weeks," he said. "That's great."

"And now you're moving to Cypress yourself."

"Yep." He caught her gaze as he drained his glass. "I'm looking forward to making friends here."

"Friends." She could just guess what kind of friends he meant. With benefits, and she wasn't going to go down that road. "I'm not cutout for the random booty call, Noah."

He slowly shook his head. "This isn't a booty call." He reached for her hand and stroked a finger over her knuckles. "And it sure as hell isn't random."

She watched his strong fingers playing over her skin and a rush of wanting struck her. "Noah."

His finger continued to move, sending sparks all over her body.

"What are you afraid of, Jessie?"

She looked up and met his eyes, which sparkled now. What was she afraid of?

At this second, looking at Noah Brady, she had no idea.

Chapter 7

Noah watched as Jessie's mind worked. Her breath was shallow and quick and her eyes flicked over his face. She nibbled that full lower lip he now knew was as succulent as it looked.

"You're a nice guy," she said.

He acknowledged that with a nod. "Yep."

"You're friends with my friends."

"I guess I am."

She licked her lips, her delicate brows drawn together. She was adorable and vulnerable, and sexy as hell. He felt like whatever he did in this moment was very important.

"It's been a long time," she admitted on a breath.

"Since?" he asked just as softly.

She reached out and traced one finger over the back of his hand where it rested on hers. Her touch was light. Hot. Perfect.

"Since I've been with a guy."

"How long?" he had to know.

She met his eyes, her eyes glistening. "Five years."

He gaped at her. "Why?" When she drew back, he gave a quick shake of his head. "I don't mean why but, Christ, look at you. You're freaking gorgeous, and sexy as hell."

His words seemed to surprise her. "You think I'm sexy?"

He ran his gaze over her thin shirt, at her full breasts and pebbled nipples he could just glimpse through the fabric. He let out a low whistle.

"Jessie, for months now I've been imagining what's under that big ugly sweater of yours. Now that I can see a little bit more of you? Yeah, you're sexy."

"You've been thinking about me?"

He cocked his head to the side. "And you've been thinking about me." He moved his hand up over her thin shirt sleeve, catching the tiny shiver he felt beneath his fingers. "I saw how you looked at me out at the model. You stripped me, baby."

A pink flush spread over her heart-shaped face, brightening her eyes now. "I did not."

He played it light, pulling his hand back as he settled into his chair. "If you say so."

She pushed at his arm, her hand lingering on his bicep. The semi-innocent touch sent heat straight to his dick.

"You stripped me first," she said. "You just admitted it."

"I couldn't help myself. I'm a guy."

She rolled her eyes and brushed her bangs off her forehead. "That's a convenient excuse."

He smiled at her. "Jessie, that's not an excuse. It's a fact."

That sent her gaze running all over him, from his chest and down his belly to where he knew he couldn't hide his reaction through his cargo shorts. He practically built a tent in his crotch.

"Is this a booty call, Noah?" she asked him flat out this time.

He gazed at her, seeing the appeal in just giving and taking what they both needed. He sure as hell needed to touch her. To taste her again. And from the heat in her eyes and the way she leaned toward him? She wanted him, too.

"No," he finally said, bringing his face to hers. "I wouldn't use you that way."

As he watched, her pupils dilated. "I know."

He tugged her out of her chair and onto his lap. Her thighs cradled him and he hissed as he grew harder. He breathed in her scent, slowly letting her fill him as he struggled for control.

"How do you know?" he asked, his lips on the pulse at the side of her throat.

She placed her hands on his shoulders, brushing her breasts against his chest. "I'm not sure, but I feel it."

He guessed she could feel more than that right now. He was throbbing against her. Cupping her face with both of his hands, he looked into her eyes. "Just let me make you feel good, Jessie.

Nothing more."

She bit her lip again and gave a tiny nod. He nearly groaned in relief. When she pressed her lips to his, sweet and plump and searching, he pulled her closer. Their tongues tangled as the heat between them ratcheted higher. She straddled him fully now, pressing along the ridge in his pants.

"Christ, Jessie." He ran his hands up and under the back of her shirt, her skin soft and silky beneath his touch. "You feel so good."

Her hands were all over him too, clutching at him like she had the other night. Tonight, though? They made their way over his belly to cup him through his shorts.

"You feel hard, Noah."

He froze, then chuckled. "You're a little bit naughty, Pixie."

She laughed softly, the sound sexy as hell. He had to touch her. He had to know just what she sounded like when she came. Lifting her shirt higher, he took his first look at her bare breasts. They were round and tipped with pink nipples. Pretty and perfect. Pinching her with his thumb and forefinger, he felt her shiver.

"Noah." She arched toward him, rising a little bit. "Oh, that feels good."

91

He slid down low enough to give her other nipple a long lick. "Sweet." Closing his mouth over her, he suckled.

Her hands were behind his neck now as she rubbed against his belly. It didn't take much maneuvering to get his hands down her sleep pants. Her panties were wet, and when his fingers touched the bare skin beneath he moaned.

"Jessie." He moved to the other breast, licking and sucking as he slipped a finger inside of her. "Christ."

Her breath hitched as she leaned back. She was close. Hell, he was almost close enough to come in his shorts. He'd make her feel good, though. He'd promised that much.

When he began to pinch her clit she cried out, so close to release. In the next instant she came, freezing as her body drew tight. Then she collapsed against him, all soft and satisfied.

"Oh, you made me feel so good," she breathed against his neck.

He held her close, willing his dick to stop pounding. He loved how she felt draped over him, her breathing soft now. For a second he thought she'd fallen asleep, until her fingers began to work on his shorts.

"Jessie." He kissed her temple, tasting the salty-sweet sweat there. "What are you doing?"

She nuzzled his neck, nibbling on his skin. "Returning the favor."

His breath hitched as she freed him, and when her hand grasped him her touch was perfect. He hadn't had a hand job since he was a horny teenager rolling around in the sand. But Jessie's touch was so damn perfect he found himself on the brink in just a few strokes.

"You like that, Noah," she said, nibbling on his earlobe. "A lot."

"Yeah, I do," he bit out.

The touch of her fingers, the press of her body, the scent of arousal, all combined to send him quickly over the edge. He shouted his release, throwing his head back with a growl.

She brought her mouth to his. "That was fun."

"Fun?" He breathed in, his pulse still racing. "Pixie, you killed me."

Her lips curved in a smile and her eyes sparkled. She was gorgeous. Sated and pleased with herself, too. The breeze kicked up and he guessed her shiver now was due to the chill in the air. He gently untangled her from his body and helped her stand. Her hair was mussed and her clothes in a tangle. Still, she deserved more than a quick grope out on the deck.

"Next time we'll use that big bed I saw in there," he told her.

"Next time?" She shook her head. "There won't be a next time."

He couldn't help but smile at her conviction, since the expression on her face told him something completely different.

"If you say so," he said, echoing what he'd said Monday night.

He came to his feet, tucking himself back into his shorts and doing a little adjusting. "I'll see you tomorrow."

"Here?" she squeaked.

He laughed softly. "No, Jessie. At the Sales Center."

"Okay. You won't tell anyone?"

"No. It's nobody's business but ours."

Her shoulders slumped in obvious relief.

He picked up the two wine glasses and went inside, leaving them on the small table. By the time she came in he was at the front door.

"Good night, Jessie."

She nibbled her lips again, those slightly-swollen lips he'd kissed but good tonight. "Good night, Noah."

He walked back to his truck and sat behind the wheel.

94

Running his hands through his hair, he tried to figure out what just happened. Yeah, they'd shared some mutual masturbation. They'd driven each other crazy with little more than their hands. There was something else, though. This girl who hadn't been with a guy in five years. She needed...something. And not just an orgasm.

He sure as hell wasn't the guy to give her what she needed. He thought back to the pleasure he'd wrung from her supple body, and was sure of one thing.

He could give her what she wanted.

***

Jessie parked her Jeep beside the Sales Center the next morning, wiping her damp palms on her khaki skirt. It was a new one, and more fitted. Her blouse was one of her usual ones, but her sweater was new as well. This cardigan was soft lemon yellow, and the buttons were little white flowers. She felt feminine in this sweater. She snorted. After last night in Noah's arms, she felt very feminine indeed.

She stepped out of the Jeep and headed for the coffee shop across the street. She'd already had a cup of coffee out at the tent-cabin but she needed an extra jolt. All night she'd tossed and turned, going over Noah's strong convictions in her head.

He said they'd be together again. He humored her with his agreement to the otherwise, but she'd seen the glint of determination in his eyes.

She'd be a fool to believe they could stay away from each other. He might find another woman to scratch his itch, but she'd never felt what she had last night with him. She couldn't give into her desires, though. For sex and for more. She'd be giving him a piece of herself, and she didn't have any to spare.

Hurrying into the coffee shop, she queued up in the order line. The morning rush seemed to be over, and she was up at the counter in just a couple of minutes. "Hey, Caro. Medium Caramel Macchiato with almond milk," she told the woman behind the counter.

"Sure thing, Jessie," Caroline said.

"Why aren't you at the bakery?" Jessie asked.

Caro tipped her head toward the skinny red-headed guy near the espresso machine. "Tom needed my help and I baked my heart out this morning so I could get away."

She smiled at the pretty baker. Caro was just a little taller than Jessie and wore her dark blond hair back in a curly ponytail. "Those pastries were a big hit yesterday, by the way. Thanks."

Caro shrugged. "Just butter, sugar and flour."

"And magic." Jessie smiled. "I couldn't begin to bake like that."

"Not over a campfire."

"Huh?"

"How's life out in the wilderness?" Caro asked.

"How did you know?" Jessie stopped, shaking her head. "Lettie."

Caro nodded. "She said you took Ty and Cassie's love shack." She gave a dramatic shiver. "I love nature, but I wouldn't think of sleeping out there."

"It's very civilized," Jessie said. "No campfire. And trust me, having a place of my own is so worth it."

Caro looked off for a second. "Must be nice. I still can't afford to move out of my parents' place."

"Your parents' place by the main lakeshore, Caro. You forget whom you're talking to."

Caro waved a hand. "Yeah, yeah. The house is huge and I have my own apartment above the garage but still."

Jessie handed Caro her card to pay. "I can get you a great deal on your own place, you know."

"Ah, spoken like one of Cypress's number one salespeople."

Jessie's brows rose. "What?"

"You're selling the hell out of the green neighborhood, according to Rick Chapman."

Jessie felt a flush of pride. "He said that?"

Caro nodded. "Sure did."

The woman behind her cleared her throat and Jessie stepped to the side. "Get back to work, slacker," Jessie said.

Caro smiled. "Try a sprinkle of salt on top of your macchiato." Then she turned her attention to the next customer.

Jessie stepped over to the side counter to wait for her coffee, mulling over what Caro said. Not about the salt, although the baker must know what she was talking about. What she marveled at was that Rick had spoken of her. That was very cool. Lettie referring to Jessie's new home as a love shack? Decidedly less cool.

Tom called her name and she took the drink from him. "Thanks."

He nodded, his face flushed. "See you, Jessie."

She lifted the lid and sprinkled a dash of salt on the caramel-marked foam and took a cautious sip. Not bad.

As she walked out of the coffee shop, she realized she was making friends here. Starting to belong. She hadn't felt like she belonged in years. Not since Dad and not since Mitch. She wondered for a second how Shannon was faring. She wouldn't let her worries about her sister interfere with the good vibes she had going right now.

"There she is," Lettie Fairfax said from her table beneath the crepe myrtle. "My favorite little Pixie."

Jessie shook her head as she walked over to Lettie. "Good morning, Lettie."

"And a good morning to you, dear."

Jessie hadn't worked in Cypress very long before she learned that Charlotte, Lettie, Fairfax was a fixture in the town center. As usual, the very Southern lady wore a large straw hat, a flower-print smock, denim overalls, and a pair of bright green Crocs. Jessie knew she was in her seventies but she looked closer to fifty. Lettie claimed this was due to healthy living, big hats and the liberal application of sunscreen. She was outrageous and sweet, and knew every bit of gossip that could be found in Cypress. Which explained just how Caro knew Jessie was living out at the far lakeshore.

"Seed time, am I right?" Jessie asked.

Lettie waved a hand over the open catalogs spread on the table in front of her. "I do love the spring." She leveled her blue eyes at Jessie from beneath the fringe of silver bangs brushing over her brow. "You know what they say about spring time, don't you Jessie?"

Jessie knew a few things but she couldn't begin to guess what would come out of Lettie's mouth. "What's that?" she asked, knowing that resistance was futile.

Lettie smiled and dropped a wink. "Why, a young man's fancy turns to love."

Jessie shook her head but she knew she was blushing. Darn her fair skin anyway. "Is that so?"

"Seems to me you should know that, living out in that love shack like you are."

"I'm alone in that 'love shack,' Lettie," Jessie pointed out.

"True, true," Lettie said. "But you never know when that can change."

A flash of her and Noah all tangled up on the back deck struck her, leaving her breathless. Oh please, she prayed Lettie would never find out about that.

Jessie tried to channel her inner Tammy, but she'd never have that kind of poise. "I'm not holding my breath," she said in what she hoped sounded flip and easy.

"Seems to me you've been holding more than that," Lettie said.

Jessie nearly swallowed her tongue. Jeez, how did the woman do that?

"W-what?" Jessie stammered.

"That gorgeous little figure of yours, dear. You've been keeping that to yourself. I say it's high time you wore clothes that fit, don't you?"

Jessie nearly fainted with relief. If anyone knew just what she'd been holding last night, she'd die of mortification. Oh, but being so close to Noah, having him touch her in that wicked delicious way and letting her do likewise was something she'd think about for some time.

"What's going through that mind of yours, Jessie?" Lettie asked.

"Hmm?" Jessie forced her attention to Lettie. "Nothing. Just working through my tour schedule."

Lettie folded her arms and leaned back. "Sure you are, honey." A familiar silver truck pulled into the lot across the street and both Lettie and Jessie watched it for a second. "Your tour schedule. Make sure and head out to the houses that handsome Noah Brady is building. Any woman would swoon to see him, and you know you sell to the wife and the husband follows."

"I know that, but how do you?"

Lettie gave her a small smile. "I have my secrets too, you know."

Jessie gave herself a shake. "I'd better head to work."

"Mmm hmm." Lettie lifted her ever-present glass of sweet tea skyward. "Have a good day at work, dear."

"And you enjoy your seed shopping, Lettie."

Jessie turned to cross the street when she heard Lettie clicking her tongue. Jessie turned to face her. "What?"

"Seeds aren't all that grow here in Cypress," the lady said in a stage whisper.

That was enough for one day. Jessie shook her head and made her way to the Sales Center, sipping her surprisingly delicious salted caramel coffee.

Chapter 8

As she neared the wide steps Noah seemed to appear beside her. He was big and close, and she could almost feel him.

"Good morning," he said, bending so that his face was near hers. "Mmm, that coffee smells good."

She clutched it with both hands. "*My* coffee smells good."

He gave her that half-smile she'd seen last night, and she tripped over her own feet.

Grabbing onto her elbow, he righted her. "Watch it, there."

She nodded, his touch reminding her of all kinds of things that shouldn't be in her head right now. "Thanks."

Tammy pushed open the door to welcome her in. "Good morning, Jessie." She eyed Noah and how he was standing very close behind Jessie. "And Noah. Hmm."

"No 'hmm,' Tammy," Jessie told her as she walked past her. "I'm going to my desk."

She trusted Noah to keep quiet about what happened last night. He'd given her his word. From what she knew about him, he was dependable. Ben was always singing his praises regarding deadlines and orders, and he was as detail-oriented as anyone Jessie had ever met.

As she neared her desk she found Oliver sitting on the edge, his arms crossed.

"Good morning, sunshine."

She glanced down at her yellow sweater and smirked at him. "Funny."

Oliver scrunched up his nose, giving her an adorable grin. "I have a favor to ask."

"What's that?"

"Would you come on my tour this morning?" he asked.

She set her coffee down on her desk and looked at him. "Why?"

"I'm touring the sisters."

Jessie could guess why Oliver wanted her to come along. For a diversion. The Atkins sisters were very active in the conservation club, and it was rare for more than a couple of weeks to go by without hearing from them. They often volunteered at the Cypress Institute filing and things like that, which freed up some of her time when she was there. They also questioned her about every person who came into the Institute, too. They weren't looking for gossip like Lettie often was, though. No. They sincerely cared about the environment in general and the property in particular.

"Which one are you most afraid of, Oliver?" she teased.

"Marge or Marigold?"

"It's a toss-up."

"Okay, you've got me," she said. "Where do they want to go?"

"The green neighborhood."

Jessie swallowed a curse. She just knew the sisters would have tons of questions for Noah. That would put her directly in his path again today, and for more than a few minutes.

She settled into her chair and opened her laptop, clicking to check her own tour schedule. "What time is your tour?"

"Eleven fifteen."

She slipped on her glasses and peered at the screen. "I have a nine thirty, but then I'm free until one."

Oliver let out an exaggerated sigh of relief. "Thank God! You saved me, Pixie. I owe you big time."

She took off her glasses and folded her arms. "They don't bite, you know."

He held up his hands. "Oh, I know. I just feel like I never have all of the information they're looking for."

She smiled. "I don't think anyone has all of the information they're looking for."

After more effusive expressions of thanks, Oliver left her to her own preparations. Her morning tour was a family of four who were interested in the more modestly-priced homes. It should be a piece of cake, and help keep her mind from taking the sisters out to see Noah and his team.

Sipping her coffee, she reviewed what she knew about this family. The kids were both boys, aged six and nine years old. She couldn't help thinking about Noah's son, Max. He really was adorable. It was clear Noah loved him, and worried about him too. It sucked that the boy didn't get to see his father during the week. She wondered about Noah's ex. What was she like? Had Noah loved her? He must have. And she must have loved him. What woman could look at him and not want him forever?

That thought made her stomach clench. The passion they'd shared last night should have left her satisfied. Heck, it was the most action she'd had in years. Truth of it was, it only made her crave more. More heat. More Noah. More of what they could be together. She had baggage. Heavy, heart-chilling baggage. He was a golden guy, with no worries except his son. He exceled at his job and everyone loved him. As for her? She had friends now but she still felt a little disconnected.

Despite her now-contentious relationship with Shannon, the sisters had been very close growing up. They'd done everything together. That was, until Dad died. Now she wondered if they'd ever be close again.

Closing her laptop, she finished her coffee and went to grab a bottle of water for the tour. Oliver was in the break room and when she walked in he gave her an adoring look, accompanied by a hand splayed over his chest.

"All right," she laughed, reaching into the fridge for a cold bottle. "I'll be back before the sisters get here."

"Anything you want, Pixie. Name it. Dinner, a bottle of wine."

She winked. "I'll keep you posted."

Her tour went as expected and, unless she missed her guess, Cypress Corners would have another new family in residence soon. As she bade the four of them farewell in front of the Sales Center, the Atkins sisters arrived early for their tour.

"Miss Wilde," the shorter of the two said in greeting.

"Jessie, Marge," Jessie corrected. "How are you today?"

"She's prickly," Marigold said with her customary smile. "Good morning, Jessie."

Marigold was tall and thin. She had a long gray-streaked braid resting over one shoulder and wore a peasant blouse with embroidered jeans and Birkenstock sandals. Marge, on the other hand, was a little bit stockier with very short salt-and-pepper hair. She wore olive green overalls, work boots and a no-nonsense expression. Jessie wasn't sure if they were blood sisters or sisters-in-law, but they were clearly as close as she and Shannon used to be.

"Are we ready for our tour?" she asked them.

"Our tour?" Marge asked. "Isn't Oliver leading us today?"

"Yes, I am," Oliver said as he joined them. "I thought you two would like it if Jessie came along."

Marigold clasped her hands. "Oh, Jessie! That would be wonderful."

"Yes, thank you," Marge put in with a short nod.

The four of them headed out to one of the golf carts parked and charged. Jessie sat in the back with Marigold while Oliver and Marge took the front.

"I'm eager to see the progress in the green neighborhood, Oliver," Marge said.

Oliver threw a worried glance at Jessie before beaming a smile at Marge. "That's where we're headed."

Marigold hummed to herself as they made their way, the vehicle bouncing as they rode over the pavement. Jessie ignored the queasiness in her belly as they neared the newest part of the development. Telling herself to pull up her big-girl panties, she looked over at Marigold.

"Did you ladies have some questions for me?" she asked.

"Not at the moment," Marigold answered. "It's the builder we want to speak with today."

"Noah Brady is a gifted craftsman," Oliver said. "All you have to do is look at the model homes and you can see how good he is at bringing the architect's vision to life.'

Marge harrumphed. "Ben Chapman has created some wonderful homes. That's true. But is Mr. Brady keeping the environment completely in his sights as he builds?"

Jessie bit down on her irritation. Giving Marge the benefit of the doubt, she leaned forward to put a hand on the woman's shoulder. "Noah is well-aware of what's at stake out here, Marge. Dr. Robbins is included in both the planning and the execution in this part of the property."

Marge nodded. "Good. It's just that Marigold and I chose to live in Cypress two years ago, over some very attractive alternatives."

"Not so attractive, Marge," Marigold put in. "That place out in Melbourne? With the manufactured homes that all looked alike?"

109

A smile teased Marge's lips. "I'll give you that," she said.

"You've seen what we do at the Institute, Marge," Jessie said. "Harmony Chapman is committed to making certain the plants are protected and Ty Walsh does the same for the animals."

"But there are more and more people moving into Cypress," Marigold said. "We can't help but be nervous about so many residents who might not care as much as we do."

"I doubt many people care as much as you do," Oliver said with just the right touch of humor.

Jessie's assurances and Oliver's natural warmth seemed to relax both sisters as they neared the green neighborhood. Bracing herself, Jessie squared her shoulders.

Oliver parked the golf cart in front of the model Jessie had visited last Monday and turned. "Ready, ladies?"

Marge gave one of her curt nods and Marigold gushed her enthusiasm. Jessie kept quiet. She just prayed she could look at Noah without thinking about how he'd felt in her hands. Of how his hands had felt on her. She just wasn't going to go there.

"Hey, there," Noah said, stepping toward them from one of the work sites.

Her gaze ran all over him, from his worn jeans that hung off his hips to the gray Henley shirt with just the right number of buttons undone. His hair was mussed, either from the March winds or from running his very capable fingers through it. Ooh, those fingers.

So much for not going there.

***

Noah tried to keep from watching Jessie as she climbed out of the golf cart. He had to focus on the other visitors. Oliver had sent him a distress signal soon after he'd seen Jessie this morning, advising him of the sisters' visit. He'd met them before and had to agree with Oliver that they were a couple of tough customers. He was confident he was up to the challenge this morning.

"Good morning," he began.

"Good morning, Mr. Brady," Marge said.

"We're so glad we could meet with you today," Marigold added.

Noah caught a look of gratitude from Oliver but it was the expression on Jessie's face that caught him. She was looking at him. Really looking at him. Christ, if she ran those eyes over the front of him one more time he'd have a lot more to explain than how the model was constructed.

"I thought we'd tour the two story first," Noah said.

He waved the sisters ahead of him, and they were followed by Oliver and Jessie. As she passed him he saw she now made a show of studying details of the model that he was sure she'd already committed to memory.

"Nice to see you again, Jessie," he said in her ear.

He'd done that earlier, spoken into her ear as he'd breathed her in. A rash of goosebumps rose on her skin, and he fought the urge to smooth them with his fingers.

She flicked her gaze back to him. "Oliver begged me," she whispered.

"What did you get in return?"

She smiled, her eyes sparkling. "I haven't told him what I want yet. Should I ask for dinner?"

He nodded. "At the tavern, I think."

"Yes. I don't expect him to treat me to the Clubhouse. I think I'll have him make it dinner for two."

"Yeah?" he asked. "Anyone in particular on the guest list?"

She shrugged as she walked past him now. "Maybe."

That one word could be taken in so many different ways, at least in his head. Would she ask him to share that victory dinner? They'd shared a kiss and a couple of orgasms, but that didn't mean they were dating. He didn't date. Ever.

He and Nadine had hooked up that one time in the parking lot of the Wild Cherry Gentlemen's Club. They'd been hot and horny, but that was all they'd shared that night. Hell, he hadn't heard from her again until a month later when she'd found out she was pregnant. It wasn't a love story. That was for sure. They both loved Max, though. That was the only thing they had in common.

As for him and Jessie, though? He wanted to find out if they had more in common than mutual attraction, no matter how smoking hot that attraction was.

He'd gotten the impression that Jessie was pretty private. He'd never heard anything about her family until she'd talked about her parent's passing. He thought Tammy had mentioned that Jessie had a sister, but he wasn't sure.

Shifting gears, he followed her and the others into the house.

"So, what would you like to know?" he asked.

Marge and Marigold turned to focus on him and he gave them a wide smile. He could get through this. He could show them just how awesome Ben's design and his build were. He just had to keep his attention from Jessie and the possibility of a date.

Jessie managed to slip past him while he showed the sisters

the backyard. There was a small pool here, and they seemed very impressed by the geothermal heating and non-chlorine filtration system. Noah hadn't built it, but he'd been damn sure there would be minimal care for the future homeowners and minimal impact on the groundwater.

"The main pool at the fitness center is heated and treated the same way," he told them.

Marge and Marigold nodded in unison.

"That was one of the features that drew us here in the first place," Marigold said with a smile. "We like our water-aerobics."

"And don't forget the hiking trails," Marge put in. "The recreation café on the trails was built to blend in with the surroundings, which we appreciate."

"That's a great example of Cypress's commitment," he said.

He knew the story well. The café was built by Rick Chapman five years earlier, and Harmony's parents ran it. In fact, the café's story was Cypress Corners lore by now. It had been one point of contention between the Institute and the development company back then, and had served to forge the partnership the two entities enjoyed today.

"I hope you're as pleased with the homes being built here,"

he added.

They both nodded vigorously, and he waved them back into the house. Oliver waited for them in the kitchen, leaning against the recycled-glass countertop.

"Where's Jessie?" Noah asked him.

"She's out in the cart."

Noah forced himself to keep from looking toward the front door. "Oh."

"Did you need her?"

Noah was beginning to think so. "Nope."

Oliver narrowed his eyes, but before he could ask a question Noah expected would be intrusive and possibly off-color, Marge and Marigold strolled back inside.

"Is there anything else?" Noah asked them.

They both shook their heads.

"Thanks for all of the information," Marge said. "Oliver and Jessie are taking us over to the east side now."

"Good," Noah said. "Lots to see out that way."

"See you, Noah." Oliver led the ladies out onto the front porch.

Noah followed them out. Jessie waved at the three of them, and then her gaze caught on Noah's. She gave him a tiny wave of goodbye, and he returned the expression with a lift of his chin.

As Oliver steered the cart away from the model home, Noah thought about that tiny wave. He'd seen a spark of something in those big eyes of hers. Was she was thinking about that "maybe," too?

He just hoped he didn't have to wait long to find out.

Chapter 9

Ben held the keys out to Noah. "It's all yours, man."

Noah took the keys and slid the signed lease agreement back across the table. "Thanks."

They sat in the main room of the tavern, toasting their agreement with a couple of cold ones. It was Tuesday night, and Noah was once again putting off the short drive home to St. Cloud.

"When are you moving in?" Ben asked.

"Before the weekend, I hope. I'd love to have Max in his new room when he visits."

"So you only get him on the weekends?"

Noah nodded. "That's the agreement. For now."

Ben arched a brow. "You want to change that?"

"I've been thinking about it. Nadine is a great mom, don't get me wrong."

"Nadine?" Ben took a sip of his beer. "Your ex?"

"No." Noah didn't tell many people this particular truth, but Ben had been a good friend from the jump. "We were never a couple."

Ben gave a low whistle. "There but for the grace of God."

That surprised Noah, since the guy was now clearly in love

117

with his wife. "Yeah?"

"I'm not proud of it, but I was pretty much a one-night kind of guy before Tammy."

Noah took a long draw on his beer. "That was my story, too."

"Was?"

Noah fingered the neck of his bottle. "I can't live that way anymore, Ben. Not with Max around."

"I get that. I know my brother Rick's son doesn't miss a damn thing."

"You got it."

"What's your...his mother's situation?"

"She's seeing a guy. Has been for a few months now."

"Are they going to get married?"

Cold settled in Noah's belly. "I don't know. I haven't thought much about that."

"Could change your custody situation."

"We don't have a custody situation. Just a parenting plan for time-sharing. School, holidays and stuff."

"I think Ty said something about that. He and Cassie take his niece Riley every weekend, but sometimes during the week now too."

"I think it would be awesome if Max could go to school here in Cypress."

"How the hell would you work that out?" Ben asked.

"No clue. Nadine's place is just over half an hour from here."

"Maybe a week-by-week thing?"

"I don't know." Noah crossed his arms and leaned on the table. "I just know I want him more often than I have him."

Ben lifted his bottle and clinked the neck of Noah's. "You'll figure something out."

Noah drank some more of his beer. "I hope so. At least I should make sure his room is all set."

"Do you need a hand moving out of the apartment?"

"That would be great, man. Can you bring your truck?"

"No problem. Will there be enough room with your truck and mine?"

"Plenty. I don't have a lot. Tomorrow work for you?" Noah asked.

"Sure. My Wednesdays are pretty light. We can head out around midday, if that works." Ben winked. "You can buy me lunch at the End Zone."

"Deal." He bumped fists with Ben. "Thanks."

They said good night, and Noah headed to St. Cloud for what he hoped was his last night sleeping in the apartment. He had the place through the end of March, but if he could get into the townhouse before then he saw no need to spend another lonely night there.

He stopped at the storage place near the apartment complex and picked up some boxes. As he packed up the place, he realized he had very little of any personal significance. He'd lived here since the fall, for God's sake. What the hell was wrong with him? It was like he was still drifting on the waves with nothing but his board between his ass and the ocean.

Except for Max's room, there was actually very little to pack. He didn't have much in the way of dishes and flatware, and he only had a couple of pans. Microwave gourmet was all he managed to do when he wasn't taking Max out to eat. Maybe he could change that. The townhouse had a gourmet kitchen, after all. He had no excuse not to use the basic cooking skills his mother had made sure he mastered.

Max's toys and a few clothes were boxed, so he stripped the twin bed and his own. His own bed was nice and big, and the only thing he'd bought for himself when he moved out here. He threw all the bedding in the wash. He'd sleep on the quilt tonight and take his bed apart in the morning.

Morning came early. He wanted to get a jump on things, and loaded what he could manage into his truck before heading out to Cypress. As he drove past the coffee shop, he looked longingly at the people streaming in and out of the place. Letting out a grunt, he turned the truck toward the townhouses instead.

They were all constructed to look like separate residences, and this village had classic details, too. Columns and railings framed the porches and deep eaves gave the homes a high-end look.

His new home was really sweet, and he knew the particulars. The end unit was just over two thousand square feet, done in soft green with cream trim and a glossy deep-red front door. It was set at the outside of the townhouse neighborhood and had views of the golf course. There was a playground just around the corner, and it was a short ride or a slightly longer walk to the shops and restaurants in the town square.

He opened the door and looked around, easily seeing the quality in the details. High ceilings and hardwood floors, an open floor plan and what looked like a kitchen that would encourage him to make more than toast and microwave mac and cheese for Max.

After moving the boxes from the bed of his truck to the floors of their respective rooms, he made his way toward the job site. The concrete block walls were being set, and the huge house was beginning to take shape. He'd all but memorized Ben's plans, and he couldn't wait to see the thing in real life.

It was always this way with him. Home construction had grabbed him early, and he'd approached his career with a determination that had surprised his dad but not his mom. She told him time and again that he could make things that would last. He scoffed at that now, as he always did. Nothing in his life lasted. Not odd jobs or relationships. Only his parents and Max, and the homes he built for other people to live in.

He reviewed the documents on the build, talked to his foreman and a couple of the subcontractors, and stopped at the model for a cup of the coffee in the minimally-stocked kitchen.

The morning flew by, and soon it was time to meet up with Ben. He parked the truck in front of the Sales Center and stepped out. To his surprise, Ben was flanked by Jake and Ty.

"Hey, Noah," Ben said. "I grabbed a couple of extra hands."

Noah blinked. "Thanks, guys."

"No problem," Jake said.

"Happy to help," Ty added. "I'll ride with Noah."

They paired up and as Noah was about to climb into his truck Jessie stepped out of the Cypress Institute and crossed the street. She looked sweet enough to eat in her light green sweater that didn't hide the body he knew she had.

"Rounded up a posse, Noah?" Jessie teased.

He grinned, gratified when her eyes sparkled back at him.

***

"I'm taking Tammy's townhouse," Noah told her.

She'd heard that just this morning, but he was moving to Cypress Corners today?

"Looks like you have plenty of help."

"Yeah. I asked Ben, but never expected this."

"Guys helping each other move?" she asked. "Isn't that in the bro code?"

Noah appeared to think that over for a second. "I guess."

Confusion was clear on Noah's face. Didn't he get that these guys were his friends? She could see that. Why couldn't he? That was another thing they seemed to have in common.

"Hmm." Tammy stood behind her now. "All that testosterone in the middle of the day? Lettie will lose her mind."

Jessie laughed and she and Tammy waved at Lettie watching avidly from across the street.

123

"I hope you have lots to move, Noah," Jessie said. "It would be a shame to waste all of that manpower."

"I don't have a lot of stuff." Noah ran a hand over his short blond waves. "I'm more worried about the amount of wings I'll be on the hook for when this is over."

Jake clapped him on the shoulder. "Hey, Ben said you're taking us to the End Zone. I think you can guess what you're in for."

Jessie stilled. They were going to the End Zone?

"Hey, don't rope them into a game of pool," Tammy told Jake. "I'd like to see my husband sometime before midnight."

"We won't be long," Ben said. He took the steps in two strides and planted a kiss on his wife's mouth. "That'll keep you."

Tammy sighed. "For a while, anyway."

Ben chuckled and rejoined the other guys. Ty climbed into the passenger side of Noah's truck as Ben and Jake saddled up in Ben's.

Noah stepped over to Jessie. "Are you busy tonight?"

She shook her head. "Why?"

"I could use your help." He glanced at the guys clearly waiting to get their show on the road before looking back at her.

"I'll get with you later."

The two big pickups roared to life and the guys drove away from the curb. Jessie glanced over at Tammy, who had obviously overheard her exchange with Noah. She wore a sly grin.

Jessie blew her bangs out of her eyes and faced her friend. "Go ahead. Say it."

"Noah asked for your help." Tammy put a hand on her hip and slowly shook her head. "Now I wonder just what you could do for him?"

Jessie flushed hot as she remembered just what she'd done for him Sunday night. "I'm sure it has something to do with his move."

"Yeah." One of her brows arched. "I'm sure he has a really big problem there."

Jessie had to laugh. "Tammy, you're bad."

"Pixie, you don't know the half of it," Tammy said, turning to go back into the Sales Center.

Jessie stood there, rooted to the sidewalk. Noah was going to the End Zone. It shouldn't matter. Lots of people went to the big sports bar in St. Cloud. Lots of guys, actually. Guys who very often ended up in her sister Shannon's bed.

Did Noah go there a lot? He was alone every night of the

week. Maybe he wasn't as alone as she'd thought? He was a good-looking guy with a strong sex drive. She knew that for sure now. He'd been so skilled as he'd given her the best orgasm in her memory Sunday night. He'd been scorching hot as he'd let go against her, too.

She gave herself a mental shake. It was only lunch. Noah wasn't going to hook up with her sister or any other woman at lunch. Besides, it wasn't like he was Jessie's guy. They weren't even dating, despite the fact that he'd angled for an invitation to dinner at the tavern. And what was that about needing her help?

"Hey there, Jessie!" Lettie called.

Jessie saw her waving and returned the gesture. It was clear that Lettie wanted to talk, and Jessie was sure the woman hadn't missed the masculinity on display just a few minutes ago. She wasn't going to fan the flames of any gossip Lettie was brewing.

"I've got to get back to work," Jessie called back.

Lettie shook her head, and Jessie imagined she could hear her clicking her tongue from where she stood. That was just the woman's too bad. Jessie wasn't going to play today.

By the end of her day, she'd managed to put any thoughts of Noah and her sister out of her head. She was being ridiculous. What were the odds?

She'd come back to the Sales Center to double-check on tomorrow's schedule, and now she shut down her laptop. She tucked it into her messenger bag, and straightened her desk. When she got lost in research she sometimes let the little things go. Not far, just far enough that she almost always had to pick up at the end of her day. Since she'd spent most of the day at the Institute, it wasn't so bad today.

Shouldering her bag, she draped her sweater over her arm and made her way down the hall to the lobby.

Tammy peeked her head out of her office as Jessie passed by. "What are you up to tonight, Jessie?"

"Nothing much," Jessie said.

"Good," Oliver added, joining them. "Then you have to put me out of my misery and tell me what you want for coming on the tour with the sisters. How about a drink?"

"Hmm." Jessie made a show of considering his offer. "What do you think, Tammy?"

"I think that the return should equal the value of the favor," Tammy said. "Just how afraid of the sisters are you, Ollie?"

Oliver shuddered dramatically. "Okay, okay. Dinner, then?"

Jessie touched her chin as she mulled that over. "Make it for two and you have a deal."

"Dinner for two." Oliver winced a little bit.

"Relax, Oliver," Jessie laughed. "I'll be happy with a night out at the tavern."

He ran back toward his desk and Tammy chuckled.

"He keeps a stash of Town Tavern gift cards in his desk drawer," she said.

"That makes it easy," Jessie said. Tammy's eyes sparkled and Jessie knew just what question she was going to ask next. She held up a hand. "I'm going to stop you right there."

"Hey, I didn't say anything." Tammy's smile was back in place, though. "It just seems to me that I could think of a perfect dinner companion to share that prize."

"Oh?"

Tammy laughed. "Pixie, you have no poker face."

Jessie bristled. "Yes, I know."

"Do you play poker?"

Jessie nodded. "My dad taught me and my sister."

"Speaking of, have you talked to her since you moved out here?"

Jessie shook her head. She wasn't about to tell Tammy about finding a nearly-naked guy in her bed. That was the last time she'd talked to Shannon.

"Not really."

Tammy rolled her eyes skyward. "If only I could have that kind of distance from my siblings."

"Your siblings are in New Jersey," Jessie pointed out.

"Calls, texts, emails…it's like they're right around the corner."

Jessie nodded toward Tammy's belly. "What about when the baby comes?"

Tammy rubbed her baby bump. "My mother told me they're drawing straws to see who comes down first. They're going to take turns helping us out." She gave a little laugh. "Ben's terrified."

Jessie shook her head. "You'll be grateful when they're here."

"Oh, I know. And I'll be grateful when they leave."

Oliver came back and handed her a twenty-five dollar gift card. "Here you go, Pixie. Highway robbery, if you ask me."

"No one asked you," Tammy put in.

Oliver huffed, and then smiled at Jessie. "Thanks again."

Jessie pocketed the card. "Have a nice night."

"You, too," Tammy said, a knowing lilt in her voice.

Jessie chose to ignore the implication.

Chapter 10

When Jessie stepped outside she was shocked to see Noah running toward her. He wore a charcoal T-shirt with faded writing on it and a pair of cargo shorts. His hair was damp and he looked a little frantic.

"Jessie," he said, skidding to a stop on the sidewalk. "I was hoping I didn't miss you."

She tried to ignore how his words made her heart give a little jump. She also tried to ignore just how yummy he looked with his clothes all messy and his cheeks ruddy, too. His eyes were almost electric blue.

"Miss me?" she asked.

"I need your help," he said.

"You said that earlier. What, exactly, do you need me for?"

He gave her a crooked smile, and the heart-jump became a flip.

"I can think of a couple of things, but right now I need your help with the townhouse," he said.

"Moving?" she asked. "I'm not exactly the big, burly type, Noah."

"No, the guys helped me and everything's there already. I took a few minutes to take a quick shower when we were done, which is why I thought I missed you."

"I still don't understand."

"I need your help furnishing the place."

"Noah, surely you can get someone better than me for that. Why don't you ask Tammy?"

He shook his head. "She and Ben have done enough for me. And I've seen how you staged some of the models, Jessie. I want the place set up like a home. Before the weekend, if we can."

"Your son will be here," she stated.

"Yep. And I want it to look good."

Her heart squeezed at his obvious sincerity. She did so love staging the houses. "Tomorrow's Thursday. When did you want to do this?"

He bit his lower lip, looking hot and adorable at the same time. "Tonight? Like, now?"

"Okay."

He grasped her arms and for a second she thought he was going to hug her.

"Thanks. Let's go over to the townhouse and you can, I don't know, get some ideas?"

Taking her messenger bag off of her shoulder, he followed her to her Jeep. She looked around the lot and didn't see his truck.

"You ran here?"

"The townhouse is just around the bend. I'm sure you've seen it when Tammy lived there."

"I went to a party there one time," she said.

She quickly flushed when she recalled just what kind of party it had been. Lingerie and toys and some other stuff she really didn't have any use for, then. Now, though? Maybe if she gave in to what she was feeling for this guy.

He put her bag in the back and slid into the passenger seat. She got in and they drove over to the townhouse. It looked a little deserted as she pulled up, and she realized that was because the homey touches like Tammy's bench and plump pillows were no longer on the porch.

"Home dull home," Noah quipped.

She smiled at him as she turned off the engine. "You'll get settled and then you'll find yourself buying things for the outside." They got out and walked to the front porch. "A bench like Tammy had. Maybe a stone frog or a dancing pig."

His eyes widened. "What?"

She touched his forearm. "I'm kidding. Look around, though. You can see a lot of your new neighbors like the cutesy little things perched around the shrubs and other plantings."

He scanned the row of units, and looked back at her. "Maybe Max might want to pick something out."

She smiled. "Sure."

He unlocked the door and waved her in ahead of him. She looked around, seeing the dark wood floors, high ceilings and architectural details like deep moldings and trim. The windows set directly to the right of the front door created a window seat in what she would say was the parlor.

"A cushion or maybe just some pillows on this window seat would make this room more cozy." She eyed the shining, very vacant wood flooring. "And how about a couch?"

He ran his hand over his hair again. "I have a couch in the great room. But I think making this a parlor might work."

"Or your office?" she suggested.

"That could work," he said.

The first floor didn't have a formal dining room, but the great room was huge. It encompassed the living area, with a fireplace faced with dark gray tile and trimmed in more creamy white molding, a substantial dining area and the gorgeous kitchen. The cabinets were white Shaker style and the counters a sparkly quartz. It was clear Tammy had chosen everything for both personal taste and resale value.

"This place is great." She walked to the linen-covered sofa, the only piece of furniture in the space besides a big flat-screen TV set on the floor next to the fireplace. "This couch is pretty nice, but you need stuff, Noah."

"Stuff?"

She nodded. "Stuff will make this place feel much more comfortable."

"What kind of stuff?"

She ran a hand over the tall counter bracketing the kitchen, the stone cool beneath her fingers. "Barstools would be the first things I'd buy," she said. "At least you and Max would have somewhere to eat. You'll need a dining table too, but we'll see what the store in town has in stock." She saw that a couple of boxes sat on the back counter. "You've got dishes and things, right?"

"The basics," he said.

"Okay. Then let's go upstairs and see what you need up there."

He arched a brow and she waved a hand.

"I told you, that wasn't going to happen again."

"That?" he asked, a slow smile curving his lips.

She had to laugh. He was so darn charming when he was teasing her. Which was, when she came to think of it, pretty much all the time since that first night they'd talked on her back deck.

"Upstairs, Noah," she said.

He waved her ahead and she climbed the polished wood stairs to the second level. A wide landing capped the top of the stairs, leading to a hallway with several doors. One door was open, and by the twin bed and Star Wars toys she glimpsed inside, she guessed that was Max's.

"Max will love this room," she said.

"I hope so. He's a pretty easygoing kid, though. He even liked his room at the apartment."

"Then let's leave his stuff alone," she said. "We won't get anything new for in here, and just rearrange things a little bit."

She directed Noah and soon the room looked bigger and more comfortable. Together they made up the bed with the clean linens Noah dug out of one of Max's boxes and the room was set. She had to admit, watching his muscles flex and stretch his shirt across his back was a great view. His arms looked pretty nice, too.

"Okay," he said, straightening to push his hair off of his

forehead. "Now my room."

She headed down the hallway to the opened double doors that apparently led to the master bedroom. And got a glimpse of a squat dresser and the largest bed she'd ever seen.

***

Noah hid his smile as Jessie came to a standstill in the bedroom doorway. He'd known when he set the bed up this afternoon that he wanted her in it.

"Is there a problem?"

She looked at him, her eyes wide. "No problem. It's a good thing this room is huge."

"This mattress is the only piece of furniture I put any thought into buying." He sat down on the edge, pressing his hands beside him. "Memory foam."

"It's nice." Her voice sounded a little weak. "You have bedding and stuff?"

He stood, grabbing the box of sheets and linens. Together they made the bed like they had Max's, but as she stroked her hand over the Egyptian cotton he couldn't help but think about having her hands on him the other night. Heat spread through him, causing his groin to tighten. Stepping back, he grabbed the quilt and tossed it onto the bed.

Jessie spread it evening, smoothing the bedding and somehow making it look fresh and welcoming. "There," she said, putting her hands on her hips.

"Right there?" he asked.

She quirked him a smile. "Ready to go?"

"Let's hit it."

They went back downstairs and she did that tilted-head thing as she surveyed the layout again.

"What?" he asked.

"I see lots of pillows in your future, Noah," she said with a smile.

"You're in charge, Jessie," he told her.

She winked. "Just remember you said that."

Grinning, he led her to the garage in back of the unit and they got into his truck. "Where to?"

"There's a retail warehouse behind the old hardware store in the city center," she said. "Just off New York Street."

He drove as she took out her phone and began to tap in some notes. He wondered if she knew she hummed as she worked. He'd caught bits of that sound before, when he'd come upon her working at the Institute, studying her laptop at her desk in the Sales Center. It was adorable, but he preferred the soft moans she'd made when she came. Just the memory made his body tighten.

They arrived at a place crammed full of furniture and accent pieces, and he discovered she was tenacious when she set her mind to something. What he thought of as her Institute outfit, sneakers, trim khaki shorts and a soft polo, were the perfect clothes for her expedition.

She led both him and the kid working there through their paces, picking out a dining set, barstools, a big chair and coffee table to add to great room, and a nightstand she said he needed in his bedroom. Pillows and a blanket were apparently next, and she paused only to ask him for a color choice.

"Blue's my favorite, Jessie," he said. "Something to remind me of the ocean."

Her brows shot up, and he saw something spark in her eyes. Crossing to a wall of pillows, she began to choose. "Let's make things feel beachy," she said. "Turquoise, cobalt. A throw in a sandy taupe."

"So blue and tan."

She smirked at him. "Trust me, these will look great with the new chair and your linen couch." She bit her lip, scanning for something.

"What are you looking for?" the kid asked her.

"I'd like some big pillows," she said. "For a deep window seat." She faced Noah. "We won't bother with a cushion. A few big pillows can be arranged as a backrest or positioned flat to make a seat."

"For the office?"

She beamed. "So that's your office? Good. Max will love hanging out there with you while you work."

Her words put the picture in his head, and he liked what he saw. His throat got thick as he imagined making a home for his son. Even if it was only for a couple of days a week right now, he knew they'd be comfortable there.

She hurried over to a maze of knickknacks and that was when he was in over his head.

"Jessie, I'm going to make a phone call."

"You don't want to pick out lamps and accents?" she teased.

"I trust your judgment."

He left her to her work and took out his phone, tapping on Nadine's number. She answered on the second ring.

"Hey, Noah," she said. "What's up?"

"Hey, Nadine. I wanted to let you know that I took a place in Cypress Corners."

"You bought a house?"

"No. I'm living in a townhouse near the town center. I think Max will love it."

"He will, I'm sure. When are you moving in?"

"I'm in. Just getting settled. Can I talk to him?"

"He's out with Paul."

Paul. Nadine's boyfriend. "Why didn't you go with them?"

"I had some stuff to do." When Noah didn't say anything right away, she went on. "They're just getting ice cream, Noah."

He wondered if she'd picked up on his possessiveness. He shouldn't be jealous of Nadine's guy. Just because he got to see Max any time he wanted to. Got to take the kid for ice cream in the middle of the week.

"Okay." He ran out of things to say, which pretty much summed up the extent of his relationship with Max's mother. "Give Max a hug and kiss for me when he gets back?"

He didn't want to say "home." He was trying to create a home for him here, and he hoped that Max would stay at Nadine's place only half of the time. If he could manage to pull that off. Today wasn't the day for that conversation, however.

"Sure thing," Nadine said.

He disconnected the call and lifted his head to find Jessie

140

standing in front of him. "Hey."

"We're all set," she said. "They can deliver the chair and dining set tomorrow, and we can take the coffee table, the barstools and the rest of the stuff."

"Stuff, huh? Well, you said I need stuff."

She laughed, the sound light. "So go and pay. Don't worry. I buy a lot of things here so they gave you my discount."

"So I owe you." He smiled. "Again."

His transaction was all but wrapped up, so he paid and he and the kid lugged bags of pillows and boxes of lamps and stuff. He closed the tailgate of the truck and shook the kid's hand.

When he and Jessie were alone, he put his hand on her shoulder. "Thanks, Jessie. I don't know how I'm going to repay you."

"You'll think of something."

The two of them climbed into his truck and he faced her. "How about dinner? It's the least I can do, tonight anyway. We can pick up a pizza at the tavern and take it to the townhouse."

"That works for me. I can't wait to see this stuff in your house."

"Not house. Home," he said. "You're helping me make the place a home."

"Home," she said with a nod.

He started the truck's engine and drove them back toward Cypress. Back toward home.

Chapter 11

Jessie swiveled on the cushioned, wrought-iron barstool to face the great room. Biting off a chunk of her pizza crust, she regarded the space. "I think the pieces we picked out will look great in here, Noah."

He refilled her wineglass, shaking his head. "You picked them out. And if they're anything like these stools, I think they'll look great."

She grinned. She couldn't help it. "Staging's one of my gifts, or so Tammy always says. It's different picking out pieces that are actually going to be lived with, though."

Noah sat on the stool next to her. "I'm looking forward to it."

"They'll text you the delivery time." She took a sip of her wine and then wiped her hands on her napkin. "Let's get started."

He chuckled and held up his hands. "Have at it, Pixie. You're the brains in this outfit."

She flushed at his praise as she hopped off the stool. She soon lost herself in pillows and accents, stepping back now and then to take in the overall effect. Pillows in blues and browns rested near the thick armrests of the linen couch, instantly

143

making the piece of furniture more inviting. The coffee table she'd picked, a whitewashed oversized plank thing that he and Max could play games on, now held a rustic lantern painted a pale turquoise, some pieces of bleached coral and a couple of starfish. A cobalt bowl of dark twig balls finished the table scape.

She ran her hands over the front of her shorts and faced Noah. "What do you think?"

He smiled as he picked up one of the starfish. "I did say ocean."

"Which I took to mean beachy." She ran a hand over the smooth tabletop. "Plus, there's still lots of room for Max to play on here."

He picked up one of the twig balls and starting tossing it up and down.

"Not with those," she said. Laughing, she caught it in the air and set it back in the bowl.

"You picked out a lot more stuff," he said.

"Yep." Crossing to the big plastic bags of pillows, she carried one over to his office. "Just a couple of pillows in here will work."

He followed behind her as she plumped the blue, taupe and

coral pillows onto the window seat. "Max will love sitting there."

"I think so," she said. "Reading or whatever as you work."

"I like it."

She smoothed the fabric of one of the big, square pillows. "I used to love to watch my dad work. He'd always have his nose in a book."

"What did he do? Your dad."

"He taught history at the high school. You should have seen how many students, past and current, came to his funeral."

Blinking the tears that almost always threatened when she thought about those dark days after his death, she turned and left the office. "Let's put out some of the accents in the kitchen."

Glass canisters, a wooden tray and three squat navy blue coffee mugs popped on the sparkly white counter. A couple of brushed metal letters, about ten inches high, propped against the white backsplash.

"You could use some greenery in here," she said. "Do you want me to get with Lettie? She'll know what you can use for a couple of easy-care houseplants."

"Sure." He touched one of the letters. "N and M. I like them."

"Good. You can hang them on this wall, between the pantry and fridge." She smiled. "I assume you know how to use a hammer?"

"Funny." He stepped beside her and looked out toward the great room. "The place looks great, Jessie."

Warmth filled her. "It's nothing."

"It isn't nothing." He took her hand in his, his thumb rubbing gently over her palm. "It's everything."

The floor shifted beneath her sneakers. She lifted her chin and fought her attraction to this man so intent on making his son happy.

"Once the big chair and the dining set get here, I think you'll be off to a good start," she said. "You'll need some artwork for the walls. Maybe some photos."

"Thanks, again."

They stared at each other for a beat, and she would just bet he could hear her heart pounding.

"I think I'm going to go," she said

"What about upstairs?" he asked.

Teasing she could handle. The other? The making-her-feel-things stuff? That was a whole lot tougher.

"I think you can manage your room, Noah."

He tugged her closer and she went pretty easily. "Maybe I think I need your help. With that bed."

She swallowed, staring up into his blue eyes. "We already made the bed."

"Yeah, we did." He moved his hands up her arms, sending goosebumps chasing over her skin. "Come and mess it up with me."

Licking her lips, she gave a tiny shake of her head. "I'm not going up there with you."

"Then stay down here." He danced her toward the now very comfy looking couch. "Mess up these pillows with me."

She sank down on the cushions, settling back against one of the new pillows. "This is very comfortable now."

He sat beside her, his big body angled toward hers. He hadn't let go of her, either. He continued to rub his hands over her arms.

"I wasn't kidding, Jessie. This means a lot, having your help with this."

Pressing her hand to his cheek, she felt the bristles there. "You showered but didn't shave."

He smiled, his cheek moving beneath her palm. "No time. I had to make sure I could sweet talk a certain Pixie into helping me."

Heat sparked between them and she tried to ignore it. "We're done now."

He turned his head and dropped a kiss in the center of her palm. "No, we're not."

He brought his sculpted lips to hers and gave her a gentle kiss.

"Noah," she breathed, her pulse beginning to race.

"Jessie," he answered, dropping his face to her neck. "You smell good. You always smell so good."

"Always?" She leaned her head back as he nibbled on the side of her neck. "When do you…smell me?"

His laugh fanned his breath across her skin. "I mean you smell sweet and hot." His tongue flicked out to tease her skin. "Perfect."

His words were powerful. No one ever called her perfect. She was too small. She was too shy. She was too…weird. Except for hanging out with her dad, she always felt just a bit out of place. Oh, but this place? On Noah's couch and in his arms? She felt at home.

The next instant she grabbed his shoulders, giving in to the sensations he was sending through her. His hands were under her shirt now, stroking her belly as he brushed right beneath her breasts. She pulled his T-shirt up, running her hands greedily over his smoothly-muscled back. She was under him now, and when his face dipped down to her belly she nearly sobbed with need.

"Your skin is so soft." He dipped a tongue in her belly-button. "Delicious."

She closed her eyes, murmuring something as he unbuttoned her shorts and eased them down her legs along with her panties. She should stop him. This couldn't lead to anything good. And then, it did.

Placing one hand under her butt, he spread her thighs with the other. "I'm going to make you come again, Jessie." He rubbed the roughness of his cheek against her inner thigh very close to her center. "I can't wait to make you come."

She bit her lip as he began to kiss her there. Hot and cold flashes struck her, making her ache for him. Her center throbbed along with her racing heartbeat as his tongue began to swirl all over every aching nerve ending.

"Oh, my," she gasped, her breath hitching in her chest. "Oh, Noah."

He kissed her belly again and suckled her clit, one strong

finger slipping inside to stroke her just right. She came a second later, bucking on his nice comfy couch as she let loose with a soft cry.

Her breathing was shallow as she slowly came back down from the high ceilings.

He was smiling at her, his face very close to hers. "You look so beautiful when you come."

His words made her heart race for a different reason. No man had ever looked at her quite the way Noah was right now. Even Mitch couldn't match the combination of sensuality and sincerity on Noah's handsome face. She knew this couldn't last. She wasn't enough for any guy to make him stick.

So she'd make sure she made him feel as good as she did. In this moment.

***

Noah could touch and cuddle with Jessie all night, but he'd seen the flicker of apprehension in her eyes. Once they'd refocused after her stunning orgasm, that was.

She shifted beneath him and he knew she had to feel how hard he was against her.

"You have to know how much I want you, Jessie."

She nodded and bit her lip, so he had to kiss her.

"Yes," she whispered. "But I can't."

It seemed like she was afraid. Not of passion, but maybe from going too fast with him. That wasn't his thing. Yeah, he took what fell in his lap but he never took what wasn't his for the asking.

"I won't force you, baby." He cupped her face, staring into those gorgeous amber eyes. "I would never force you."

She lowered her lids, as if she was hiding from him. "That's what he always said."

He froze. "Who?"

She looked at him again, her gaze soft. "He doesn't matter." She ran her hands over his back like she had before. "He hasn't mattered in a long time."

When she reached between them to grasp him, he nearly growled.

"Jessie, you're going to kill me." He sucked in a breath as she squeezed. "Again."

Smiling, she unbuttoned his shorts and he nearly came as she studied him. "I don't know how to do what you did to me, Noah. With your mouth."

She sure could kiss. That much he knew. The image of her sucking his cock nearly sent him over the edge. Those soft, full lips. That talented little tongue.

"You want to?" he asked.

She nodded. "I'll have to learn how. I'll figure it out."

"I just bet you will." Closing his eyes, he focused on her fingers stroking him just right. "Keep doing what you're doing right now, and you can worry about your mouth later."

She let out a soft little laugh, and the fear he'd felt from her seemed to dissipate. "You're close, Noah."

He pressed up on his hands to brace himself. She had both of her hands on him now, teasing and tempting, and he knew he'd come in a second.

He shuddered, everything pulling tight. "So close."

Shifting, he pulsed against her hands. Then he came, hard and hot and so right against her bare belly. She looked up at him through her long lashes, a flush of pride on her face.

"When you look at me like that, Jessie." He blew out a breath. "Damn."

She reached up for him. She touched his face, and then drove her fingers through his hair. "You look pretty darn hot yourself."

He laughed, and then used his shirt to wipe her belly. Kissing her parted lips, he relaxed his arms and held her close.

"You made me weak."

"Strength is overrated," she said.

Moving, he sat down on the couch and tugged her up to lean against him. "Do you want to talk about it? You know, the guy?"

Her lips thinned as she shook her head. "No. I stopped thinking about him years ago. I won't waste any time talking about him now."

"I could kill him for you." He rubbed her arm as he pulled her closer. "Or at least break his legs."

"Thanks, but that's okay." She patted his thigh. "I'm okay."

"You sure? I know when they're pouring concrete next."

She laughed now, that bright easy sound he so liked. "I'd hate to see you go to jail."

He laced his fingers through hers, holding her hand against his leg. "Yeah, I don't want to talk to Max through a wall of glass."

They sat like that for about a minute and then she stirred.

"I should get home."

She got up and straightened her clothes. Her hair was a mess and she looked so cute he wanted to see just how messed up he could get her.

"Do you ever get lonely out there?" he asked.

She seemed to think for a second, and then shrugged. "It's nice and quiet, and that's what I want right now."

"You have my cell number, right?"

"Yes."

He stood and wrapped his arms around her. "Give me a call if you get lonely." He dropped a kiss on her temple. "And not just for a booty call, although I'd answer in a heartbeat."

She patted his chest, leaving her hand resting right over his heart. "Will do."

He saw her to the door and waited while she got into her Jeep. It was dark now, and as she drove away he watched her taillights heading toward the town center. Shutting the door, he looked around the townhouse. Jessie seemed to be everywhere, in the things she'd picked out and placed but especially in the messed up pillows on his couch.

She'd been afraid there in his arms. When she'd said she couldn't. Some guy, some bastard, hurt her and made her think she couldn't have sex? She sure as hell could. Hell, she could just look at him and make him come.

He went into the kitchen to wash up, and then began to unpack his dishes and things. She'd done it. Just like he'd believed she would. The townhouse felt like a home, and he couldn't wait to bring Max back here on Friday.

He might not know what had happened between her and that asshole in her past, but when Jessie got into his bed, and she would get into his bed, he'd make certain that she wanted to. With him. He smiled to himself.

He'd make her feel safe right before he made them both feel so damn good.

Chapter 12

By the time Friday afternoon rolled around, Jessie was ready for the weekend. Yesterday afternoon Noah had sought her out and made a point of telling her how great the new furniture looked. He'd thanked her again, and she was tempted to ask him to dinner on Oliver's gift card. In the end, she hadn't. There was just something about the pull between them that put her on her guard. She had trouble focusing when he was around, too. Trouble thinking, really.

Hadn't she told him out at the lakeshore that they wouldn't fool around again? And yet, they had. She'd loved everything he'd done to her with those hands and that mouth. She'd wanted to kiss him…there, too. She'd been sincere when she'd said that, and the hunger on his face told her he'd be more than fine with that. It was just that she really didn't know how to do it. Maybe she'd do some online research this weekend. She laughed to herself. Just imagine what kinds of ads would show up in her social media newsfeed after that little project!

She shut down her laptop and began her ritual of straightening her desk. As she packed up, she thought back to what she and Noah had talked about. Jeez, she was mortified every time she thought about how she'd gotten scared there for a minute. How could she even think about Mitch when she was with Noah?

Mitch had been a stalker. A controller. A bully. He'd check on her all the time, look into her search history online and thumb through her phone. He hadn't liked it when she went anywhere with the people she worked with, so she'd stopped accepting their invitations until they didn't ask anymore. He didn't even like her hanging out with Shannon, which served to drive a deeper wedge between her and her sister. Five years later, they just didn't have the comfort and closeness that she saw among all of the Chapman siblings.

She'd been with Mitch for four long months before he'd gotten tired of her. Belittled her. Told her she wasn't worth his time. She'd cried that day, but not because she would miss him. No. That day was the best day of her life.

She put her laptop in her bag and stood, rolling her chair back under the desk. As she walked down the hall toward the lobby she ran into Tammy coming out of her office.

"Hey, girl," Tammy said. "Noah told Ben you were a big help with the townhouse."

"It was my pleasure." Her cheeks heated at the double-entendre but she tried to ignore that. "The place was gorgeous with nothing in it, though. It was very easy dressing it up."

Tammy smiled. "Yeah, I had a blast picking out every little bit of the place when it was being built." She winked. "I got to do that with our house out in the green neighborhood, so I'm okay with giving my old place over to someone else."

"I think Noah's son will love it," Jessie said. "Lots of nooks and crannies to tuck himself into, and plenty of space to play."

"I'm dying to see what you've done with it," Tammy said. "Ben and I are thinking about stopping by tomorrow to take him a housewarming present."

"That would be nice."

"You should come, too," Tammy said.

Jessie waved a hand. "Oh, I don't think so."

"Why not? Isn't Noah your friend?" Tammy narrowed her eyes. "Or are you more than friends?"

"Tammy, stop," Jessie said. "I helped him furnish his new house. That's all."

"If you say so."

Jeez, she was getting tired of that little phrase. Noah said that every time she told him they weren't going to kiss. Or fool around. Or anything more.

Jessie thought for a second. "You know, I was going to ask

158

Lettie for some houseplant suggestions for Noah's place. I guess I can take a few of them over tomorrow."

"You see?" Tammy grinned. "Was that so tough?"

Jessie rolled her eyes. "What time are you heading over there?"

"Not sure. Ben's going to text him and find out when he'll be around. I'll let you know."

"Thanks," Jessie said. "I'll see you tomorrow, I guess."

Tammy nodded and Jessie made her way through the lobby.

"Have a nice weekend, Jessie," Ty's mother said from her perch behind the front desk.

"You too, Sharon," Jessie said. "Is Riley coming over?"

Sharon lit up with a smile at the mention of her four-year-old granddaughter. "Yes. Ty and Cassie are going to get her and she's sleeping at our house."

Jessie nodded. She knew that Sharon lived with Ty and Cassie in Cypress, but Ben was designing a house for the couple in the green neighborhood. Jessie was grateful that they let her have the tent-cabin months before their house would be ready.

"I'm sure you'll have a blast," Jessie said.

Sharon grinned. "That girl is such a little spitfire! She's so much like Cassie you would think they were blood."

Jessie laughed. "Good night, Sharon."

"Good night, dear."

Jessie stepped out onto the walk and felt a wave of loneliness overtake her. It was true she had more friends now than she'd had before she worked here. It was also true that she felt those friends getting closer with every passing week. Friends of friends, their family members, their neighbors. It had to have something to do with this place.

Cypress Corners fostered a sense of community she'd never felt before. When she'd lived with Shannon and their father, they didn't really socialize much with the people who lived on either side of their house. Dad was friendly with his students and other faculty members. Shannon hung out with her boyfriends and, later, her hookups. But Jessie had just kind of existed. She'd been content to simply live on the sidelines. Her mess of a relationship with Mitch just served to widen the space between her and other people around her.

Now she found she liked talking to the people she'd come to know in Cypress. Lettie. Harmony. Tammy and Oliver. Noah. Grabbing dinners with them. Attending family events, like Harmony and Rick's picnics. It was all so nice. There wasn't another word for it, really. It was nice, and she was starting to feel like she belonged.

The thought of heading right out to the tent-cabin didn't hold its usual appeal. It was nearly five thirty, so she walked over to the town market to pick up a few groceries. Cooking at her place didn't give her much of a challenge, though. The world's smallest oven and a two-burner cooktop didn't invite much experimentation. She'd cooked for Shannon and her dad, although after he died Shannon didn't make it home for dinner very often. She chose to drink her meals, mostly. A pang of guilt struck her and she drew out her phone.

Settling on one of the carved metal benches set beside the walk, she thumbed through her contacts until she located her sister. Tapping the screen, she placed the call.

Shannon's light and teasing voice came on as the call went straight to voicemail. Closing her eyes, Jessie took a breath and left her message.

"Hey, Shannon. It's Jessie. Just checking in." She paused. "Give me a call when you get the chance? Talk to you soon."

She disconnected and stared at the screen. Shannon was probably working. It was a Friday, and the End Zone was usually hopping. Between the many TV screens broadcasting everything from Ultimate Fighting to fishing, the attached pool hall and long fully-stocked bar, the place did a great business. Jessie hadn't been there in months, though. Her relationship with Shannon was so strained it was just easier to keep that distance.

Going into the market, she picked up a basket and began to grab a few things for dinner. Rice was easy, and a stir fry, so she picked up a package of fresh chicken tenderloins and some small sweet peppers. A bottle of wine to sip on her back deck. Alone, of course. Noah had Max with him, and she couldn't expect him to come over just because they'd messed up his new pillows.

She spied a tousled blond head out of the corner of her eye and turned to see Noah's son on his tiptoes. He was peering into the ice cream freezer, his eyes searching for the perfect treat.

"Just pick one, buddy," Noah said.

He was wheeling a small two-tiered shopping cart that held a carton of milk, some cereal, bread, lunchmeat and a couple of boxes of macaroni and cheese. He looked good, too. Worn jeans and a dark blue Henley shirt that both did really nice things on his build.

"Hey, Noah," she said.

He looked up in surprise, and then a wide smile spread across his face. "Jessie, hi."

Max looked over, his eyes wide. "Hi!"

"Hi there, Max," Jessie said.

Max nodded, and then once more fell victim to the lure of ice cream. "I want the chocolate one, Daddy."

"Okay." Noah slid the glass top to one side and drew out the chocolate-coated mess-making frozen pop. "I guess you deserve a treat before dinner."

"Yay!" Max hurried over to counter. "Come on!"

Noah stood with Jessie for a minute, and she took the opportunity to smirk at his shopping cart.

"What?" he asked.

"Nothing. Just wondering at the meals you guys will have this weekend. Cereal, sandwiches and mac and cheese?"

"That's really all a guy needs, Jessie." He lifted his chin toward her basket. "Looks like you plan to cook."

"Yeah, Noah. It's called having a meal."

He gazed longingly at the meat and vegetables, and shot a look at his meager selections. "You know, I have a big kitchen in my new place."

She could just guess what he was thinking behind that small smile of his.

***

Noah watched as Jessie's eyes danced with humor. He liked

this Jessie, too. Teasing Jessie.

"Yes," she said with a soft laugh. "I seem to recall that."

"How would you like to come and cook for us?"

"Us?"

"Me and Max and you." He chuckled. "Come on, Jessie. Don't make me beg. You know, a home-cooked meal would make the townhouse feel more like a home."

"Oh, that's playing dirty." She nibbled her lip, and then gave a nod. "All right. Let me go grab a couple more things."

"It seems I just keep asking you for favors," he had to admit.

"I don't mind. Cooking for you and Max beats cooking for myself."

Relieved, he grabbed her basket and transferred her items to his cart. "The supplies are on me, since you're providing the labor."

"Spoken like a builder," she teased.

She picked up another package of chicken, a bottle of olive oil and a few jars of seasonings and met up with them at the counter.

"How do you know I don't have oil or spices?" he asked.

She smirked. "Sandwiches and mac and cheese, Noah?"

"All right, you got me."

Max was practically hopping up and down as he waited for the cashier to total Noah's purchase.

"Here." Noah handed Max his pop as soon as he finished paying. "Before you burst into flames."

Max giggled and Jessie smiled at the exchange. Stepping out onto the wide brick-lined walk, they headed for his truck.

"I have to get my Jeep," she told Noah.

"Okay. Max and I will bring the groceries back to the house."

"She's coming with us?" Max asked.

"Yeah, buddy. Jessie's going to cook for us."

He could tell that Jessie braced herself for some sort of small-boy dismissal, but Max grinned. "Oh, good."

Damn, he loved the boy. "I think he might be a little tired of guy food."

Jessie smiled and walked back toward the Sales Center. Noah buckled Max into his seat and they drove back to the townhouse. He realized that he'd never had a woman over to the apartment when Max was over. Not that he'd had many woman over to begin with. He preferred to keep his game limited to road trips, but it had been months since he'd played.

"So you're okay with Jessie coming over to the house?" he

asked Max as he drove.

"Sure. She's nice."

It was a simple statement but Noah had to agree with him.

By the time they were toting the groceries into the townhouse, Jessie was pulling up in her Jeep. She smiled at Max and took the bag he was holding.

"So do you like chicken, Max?" she asked.

"It's okay."

She shared a look with Noah above his son's head, and he dipped his head. Max ran up the stairs and disappeared into his room.

"I take it he likes his room?" she asked as she began to unpack the bags.

"Yep." He took the cold stuff she handed him and stowed it in the fridge. "We came here when we first got back from Melbourne."

"Do you usually pick him up early?"

"I only get him on the weekends. I arrange my schedule so I can cut out for the coast by four the latest."

"And you don't mind my being here?"

"I asked you here, Jessie. And you're cooking for us."

She appeared relieved, and began to pull open a couple of

drawers until she found a knife. Washing her hands at the sink, she glanced around. "Do you have a cutting board?"

He reached into one of the bottom cabinets and set it on the counter. She rinsed the peppers and started to peel the onion. "The place really looks great, Noah. Are you happy with your choices?"

"My choices?"

She smiled. "Okay, are you happy with *my* choices that you agreed with?"

"Completely."

She began to rinse and slice the little peppers and the onion. "I need a pot and a frying pan."

"I have those."

"See? You're not completely clueless."

"I know how to cook, Jessie. I just don't care to."

She shook her head and set about making the rest of their meal. Max came tumbling down the stairs just as the smells of fragrant oil mixing with the peppers and onions filled the air.

"Mmm!" Max said, climbing up on one of the barstools to watch what Jessie was doing. "It smells like pizza."

"I'll take that as a compliment," Jessie said as she added the chicken to the pan.

Noah managed to measure out the water as she instructed and the rice was soon simmering on the stove.

"Come and set the table with me, buddy," he said to Max.

He and Max set out his plain dishes and utensils. Soon they were serving up the rice, which he had to admit he'd cooked perfectly, and the chicken and vegetables she'd made.

"This is fantastic," Noah said around a mouthful of food, not apologetic in the least that he was stuffing his face. "Damn. Oops. Darn. Sorry, Max."

Max shrugged and ate a good portion himself, for a kid. Jessie seemed to bloom under Noah's compliments. Didn't she realize how incredible she was? She seemed to do everything just right.

They cleaned up together as Max played on the coffee table with his Star Wars guys. He nudged Jessie with his elbow. "Just like you said."

She grinned. "Hey, I was a kid once you know."

They shared another smile. He liked this. Having another adult with him, and a pretty hot one at that, as he and Max started another weekend together. The food was just an added bonus.

When she left he missed her. Flicking on the big screen, he

settled back as Max continued to play.

"So do you like Jessie, Max?"

"Yeah. She's nice," Max said simply.

He continued to play and Noah traveled through the channels. Max made little sounds for his guys, mostly blasting each other. He stopped playing for a second and looked up at Noah.

"Hey, Daddy?"

"What?"

"Is Jessie your girlfriend?"

Noah chose his next words very carefully. He didn't know what he and Jessie were, actually. They were friends who shared a little bit more than conversation, but he couldn't tell his six-year-old son that.

"She's a girl and she's my friend," he finally answered.

"Are you going to marry her?"

He gaped at his son, completely at a loss. "Why do you ask that?"

"A lot of my friends have a mom and dad who are married. Nick's mom and dad are married."

"That's true." Worry tingled up the back of Noah's neck. "Is this something your mom talked to you about, buddy?"

169

The boy shook his head. "No. I asked Paul about it when we went out for ice cream."

"And what did Paul say?"

"He said something like you said. He really likes Mommy."

Relief nearly made Noah groan. "Uh huh."

In the next second Max was back to playing and Noah was doing his best not to freak out. So Paul and Nadine weren't planning on getting married any time soon. Noah didn't know anything about the guy and, if he was going to be a permanent fixture in Max's life, that had to change. He also didn't like the idea of another man spending so much time with *his* son.

He had to talk to Nadine, though. About that and about maybe sharing more of Max's time now that Noah had a home.

He *was* building a home here. For Max on the weekends, anyway. The kid's questions about Jessie, and about marriage of all things, really gave him pause. He was playing at something with Jessie. That was for sure. But, what?

He didn't feel like it was the time in their...whatever this was to have that conversation. Did she want to date? Did she want more than a few heated nights together?

A bigger question loomed, though. Just what the hell did he want?

Chapter 13

Jessie tossed her empty yogurt container in the bin by her desk, adjusting her glasses as she peered at her laptop. It was Monday afternoon, and it looked like she had nothing else scheduled today. She glanced at the filing cabinet behind her, reasoning she could reorganize the guest comment cards to get ready for the email push they were set to do in a couple of weeks.

"Hey, Jessie."

She looked up to see her boss walking toward her desk. "Hey, Rick. What's up?"

"You don't have any other tours this afternoon, right?"

"Nope. Why?"

"If I give you the rest of the afternoon off, would you take a tour tomorrow around five?"

"Sure."

Rick smiled. "Thanks. My father sent a couple of guys down here to check things out. They're staying at the inn."

"From Chapman Financial?"

Rick rolled his eyes. "Yeah. It seems that Bill's grooming them to take the positions Jake and I wouldn't touch with a ten-foot pole."

Jessie thought for a minute. She knew both Rick and Jake had little to nothing to do with their father, Bill Chapman. Jessie had met him more than once. She could admit to herself that he was full of bluster and confidence, and that he scared the crap out of her.

"Your father isn't coming, is he?" she asked.

"Not this time. I want to give these guys the full-court press on Cypress while they're here, though."

She turned and ran her hands over her skirt. "But why me? Tammy would be the best one for the job."

"That's debatable, but I don't want any Chapmans along for the ride."

"Why?"

Rick leaned against her desk and crossed his arms. "Who knows what kind of instructions Bill gave these guys, Jessie? I don't want them anywhere near anyone named Chapman."

Jessie wondered at the strange relationship all four of the Chapmans had with their father, and gave a silent prayer for the very wonderful man who had been hers.

"You've got me, Rick."

He gave a curt nod. "Good. You and Noah take them through the neighborhoods and over to the east side."

A nervous tingle went through her. *Noah?*

She'd gone over the evening spent with Noah and his son. Over and over again. The domesticity. The comfortable, at-home sensation. It was so tempting to think she could have that. It was what she'd craved after her dad died. It was probably why she'd been drawn to Mitch back then. She'd longed for that sense of family, and believed him when he'd said he could give it to her. It was what she was beginning to crave now with Noah, and she couldn't allow herself to think she'd actually have that fantasy.

That was the reason she'd begged off accompanying Tammy and Ben when they paid a housewarming call at Noah's new place on Saturday. Thank goodness it was via text, because Jessie suspected Tammy would have seen right through Jessie's thin excuse. Housework? Really? She could clean the entire tent-cabin in less than half an hour. She'd thrown in laundry as an added duty, and called it a day.

Setting aside her pipe dreams, she focused on the job at hand. "Noah's coming with me? Why?"

"He's our newest builder, and the green neighborhood is the hottest ticket right now."

"True."

"And I'm counting on you to bring home the eco side of

things, Jessie."

"Will do."

"I'll let them know you'll meet them here at five tomorrow."

She nodded. "Okay."

He turned to leave. "So get out of here," he said over his shoulder.

Laughing to herself, she shut down her laptop and tidied her desk. It wasn't even two o'clock, so she considered just how she would occupy her free afternoon. Waving to Lettie across the street, Jessie headed for her Jeep. She might be off every weekend, but free time on a Monday felt like a luxury.

"You're getting spoiled," she told herself.

When she used to work retail her schedule changed every week and she almost never had evenings or weekends off. Yes, she was giving a tour to some Boston corporate types tomorrow evening. Having Noah there would serve as a distraction, but with Bill Chapman's people to concentrate on she'd make it through.

Noah was still on her mind as she picked up a few things at the market and then parked in front of the tent-cabin. Chickening out of visiting him on Saturday had made her feel a little bit foolish all day. Oh, what he'd made her feel that night she'd helped him decorate! When she'd been over Friday night, it had taken all of her willpower to keep from envisioning that and more on his couch. Saturday she'd done a little online research, though. Naughty research. If she ever tangled with Noah again, and she suspected she would, she wanted to please him as he'd pleased her.

Her pulse spiked as she recalled all that she'd learned on her little foray into internet erotic instruction. She'd never been very comfortable with the sexual side of things, and Mitch hadn't encouraged it. He'd wanted what he wanted when he wanted it, until she began to dread their intimate time together. But with Noah? He was the most beautifully-built man she'd ever seen, but it was that crooked smile and those crystal blue eyes that made her want him.

She decided what she would do with her afternoon. It had been about two weeks since she'd run more than just a couple of miles, and today was perfect for a longer run. It wasn't too hot today and there were several clouds in the sky. That was no surprise, since rain was expected around dinner time. Living in Florida, a person got used to checking the hourly weather forecast. Heck, she had an app on her phone just for that. Giving

175

outdoor tours, and living out by the lakeshore, she wanted to know what was coming her way. Forewarned was forearmed, after all.

Humming, she went into the tent cabin and changed into what she considered her running uniform. Brightly-patterned leggings, sports bra, fitted tank top imprinted with a cheeky yet inspirational saying, and cushy socks.

As she smoothed her hands over her thighs, she realized that the clothes were just about as close-fitting as they could get. Maybe she'd been ready for a change earlier that she'd thought, since she'd been wearing these kinds of running clothes for months now. She'd slather on some sunscreen too, of course. Just because it was cloudy didn't mean there wasn't a burn risk.

After pushing her short hair back with a wide, soft headband, she laced up her running shoes and grabbed her water belt.

"Just one today," she said as she filled the bottle from the sink.

She figured she'd run just over six miles today. A 10K would take her under an hour, which would get her back home before the rain if it decided to come earlier than forecasted.

She set her sports-tracking watch, donned her sunglasses

and stretched her legs. As she mapped her route in her head, she made the decision to avoid the green neighborhood. It was enough that she'd be spending time with Noah tomorrow after hours. Again, even though it would be all business. She didn't have to run into him today. Literally.

Stepping outside the tent-cabin, she began to run over the sandy path toward the town center.

***

After Noah checked on site prep for the latest house to be built in the green neighborhood, he drove to the Sales Center to get with Ben on some specifications.

He waved a hello to Ty's mother and walked straight back like he usually did. Or so the woman had said after he'd crashed into Jessie that morning a couple of weeks ago. Ben's office was about halfway down the corridor toward the larger office where Jessie worked, but he forced himself to the task at hand.

Stopping at Ben's open office door, he poked in his head. Ben sat at his desk, focused on his computer screen.

"Ben, do you have a minute?"

Ben looked over. "Sure, man. What's up?"

Noah stepped in. "I wanted to double-check on the specs for lot fourteen."

177

"Lot fourteen. That's the narrow two-story." Ben nodded and clicked to pull up the documents. "What do you need to check in particular."

"The stem wall is being built, but I thought of something. Is there anything indicated for this build regarding the west-facing wall?"

Ben stared at him for a minute, and then his brows shot up. "There's no natural shade to the west of that lot. Nice catch."

Noah shrugged and sat in the chair facing Ben's desk. "It's a two-story on a corner, but without a barrier that side of the house will get very hot."

"And lead to higher A/C usage and cost," Ben added. "What do you suggest?"

"I know the environment was very different out on the east coast, but several of the houses I built out there had similar orientation. Sandy soil meant not many shade trees."

"What did you do?"

"Limit the windows on the west-facing side of the house, actually."

Ben narrowed his eyes, and Noah guessed he was envisioning the elevation of the house in question. "That could work. I set the laundry room on that side, as well as the half-bath. I could substitute a narrow window for the one in the laundry, and the bathroom wouldn't need a window since we're equipping it with a vent fan."

"And maybe order windows with a reduced solar-heat gain coefficient for the remainder of that side of the house," Noah said.

"I assume they make them in a style that would be indistinguishable from the other windows specified?" Ben asked.

"Yep."

"Let me add that substitution into the materials list for that house." Ben typed on the keyboard, throwing Noah a grin at last. "Nice catch, man. I'll go over the upcoming lots to be built and see if any others have similar concerns."

"Cool."

"Just get me the specifics on the windows for the materials list?"

"Will do." Noah stood. "Thanks again for stopping by this weekend. Max loves the sling chair you got him for his room."

"That's great."

"And the smoker? Above and beyond, man."

Ben smiled. "I expect to be invited over for ribs. They're the only thing my brother can't make."

Noah chuckled. "There'll be a learning curve, but I promise you and Tammy will be the first people I have over."

"Just me and Tammy?"

Noah leveled a look at him. "Who else?"

"Jessie. She was supposed to come with us on Saturday, you know. Tammy said she had something else to do at the last minute, though."

That thought brought Noah up short. "Oh," was all he could think to say.

"Thanks again for coming in with this, Noah."

"I'll leave you to it, then," Noah said.

He left the Sales Center, but didn't head back to the green neighborhood. Instead, he turned the truck toward the far lakeshore. He wasn't looking for Jessie. He was pretty sure she was still tucked behind her desk. Hiding behind her laptop. Hiding from him. That last thought felt a little mean-spirited but, seriously, she had something more important to do on Saturday than come over to his place with her friends? He thought the two of them were becoming friends, too.

As he reached the end of the pavement where the path to Jessie's place began, he parked the truck over on the side of the road. The sky was getting dark, and fat clouds seemed to roll in out of nowhere. Stepping out, he walked around to the side and leaned against the truck, staring at the thick copse of trees bracketing what would one day be another recreation center. It was nearly dead quiet out here. No road traffic. No construction.

The tent-cabin wouldn't be disturbed for some time, since the new construction would be on the other side of the lake. Rows and rows of active-adult homes would go up to the southeast as well. Mr. Forbes had talked to Noah about being involved in that project, but that decision was a ways off yet.

Jessie's place would remain hers for a while, then. A curl of want settled in his belly. He'd loved sitting out with her on that back deck. That first time just talking. The next, messing around. Wednesday she'd come through for him, helping him begin to make a home for Max. What they'd shared on the couch, the way she'd felt and what she tasted like as she'd come apart, was something he wouldn't forget for a while. She'd come over and cooked for him and his son, damn it. Why the hell hadn't she wanted to come over on Saturday for a friendly visit?

A sound reached his ears, a soft pounding like footsteps growing closer. He turned his head to see a small figure running toward him. He couldn't see the runner's identity from here, but as she drew closer it was clear she was a woman. And damn, she was built. Long legs for her short stature and breasts high and round beneath her tank top. Big sunglasses covered half her face and as she neared she kept her gaze on the road in front of her.

He walked around to the back of his truck and leaned against the tailgate. When the runner was about thirty feet away, he could see her better. She kind of looked like Jessie, but he couldn't be sure. He had to have conjured her up with his dirty little mind. He seemed to see her everywhere.

Just last Wednesday when he'd thought that one of the other servers at the End Zone looked like her, too. With dark hair, but with a Pixie face a lot like Jessie's. He hadn't mentioned it to Ben or the other guys. He could just imagine what they would have said if he'd been all, "hey, doesn't that girl look like Jessie?"

The runner stopped, tossing her head back as she breathed through her open mouth. Her hands were on her narrow waist now, further accentuating her curves. When she took off her sunglasses and peered closely at the fitness watch on her wrist, it seemed like she almost couldn't read it. Recognition slammed through him. It was her.

Jessie.

Chapter 14

Jessie pushed her sunglasses up on top of her head and squinted at the watch she'd paused. Six point one miles on the dot. She was pretty happy with her pace, having finished the 10K in just under fifty-seven minutes. Walking in a large circle, she closed her eyes and took deep breaths as she brought her heartbeat down. She was drenched with sweat but she felt really good. Grabbing her water bottle out of its holder in her belt, she sucked down a long swallow.

She studied the gravel-strewn pavement as she made her way toward the turnoff to the tent-cabin, mindful of slipping or maybe twisting her ankle. Lifting the hem of her tank top, she mopped her face. A low whistle brought her up short. Her head jerked up and she saw Noah leaning against the back of his truck.

"Noah," she said, sucking in another breath.

"Damn, Jessie," he drawled.

She blinked, and then looked down at herself. Dropping her tank top back over her abdomen, she ran a hand over her brow.

"What are you doing out here?" she asked.

He crossed his arms, and she couldn't help but notice how nice those arms were. His sleeves were pushed up and his shirt stretched across his chest and shoulders. Her pulse kicked, and she knew it had nothing to do with her run.

"I drove out here to think, I guess," he said. "I met with Ben earlier and didn't need to go back to the green neighborhood."

She nodded, at a loss. His gaze ran all over her and she fought the urge to cross her own arms and hide from his eyes. He'd seen her half-naked, after all. He'd touched and kissed her breasts, and more. She shivered.

"How far did you go?" he asked.

"Ten K."

He nodded. "I run, too. We'll have to run together sometime."

"I don't think so." She smiled, taking a sweeping glance at his very long legs. "You'd leave me in the dust."

"Maybe." He straightened away from the truck's bumper. "What's your pace?"

"Around nine minutes today."

He grinned. "I think we'd do just fine together, Jessie. In sync."

She thought about their couch clutch again, and knew he outpaced her sexually too. She hid her smile now. She'd read up a bit this weekend, hadn't she? Maybe she could close the gap.

"What's your plan for your Monday night, Noah?"

He shook his head. "Not a thing, Pixie. You?"

"I'm going to shower. Then sit on my back deck and watch the sunset."

His eyes glittered. "Sounds nice."

"What to join me?"

He winked. "In the shower?"

She laughed. "In your dreams."

He ran his gaze over her again. "Most definitely."

She dipped her head, feeling a rush of a whole different kind of heat now. "I'll meet you there."

"You don't want a ride?"

"I'm a sweaty mess, Noah."

"Believe me, I have no problem with that."

Shaking her head at him, she turned and started jogging toward home. "I'll meet you there."

"Take your head start, Pixie. I have no problem keeping up."

She nearly stumbled over that line. Home was less than half a mile from the turnoff, and she made it up on the front porch as Noah's truck made its slow-paced way to a spot near the trees bordering the small yard.

She took the key out of her running belt and unlocked the front door as he stepped out of the truck and walked toward her. "Come on in."

He stopped before stepping up on the porch, looking up at her through his lashes. "You sure?"

She had a moment to consider what was going to happen here tonight. She had no illusions. She and Noah were going to fool around again. Just how far around, she wasn't as certain.

"Yes," she stated.

That crooked grin curved his delectable mouth. "Thank God. Otherwise I'd have to use your shower after you. Ice cold."

Grinning, she went inside and gathered her things for her shower. "Make yourself at home. I won't be long."

Slipping on her rubber boots, she clomped out to the shower. By the time she returned, fresh and still a little damp, Noah was stretched out on her bed. His arms were up and his hands folded beneath his head. His ankles were crossed and his big booted feet hung just over the edge of the mattress. Very big feet. No surprise there.

"Um, I have to get dressed," she said, holding her towel clasped between her breasts.

"Not on my account, you don't."

A flush spread from her chest up over her face. "Never mind." She pointed a finger at the little fridge. "As comfortable as you look laying on my bed, why don't you open the wine?"

He swung his legs around and stood in one smooth motion. "You got it. White?"

"Tonight, yes. I'm making a cold crab salad."

He made a soft growling sound as he crossed to the fridge. "That sounds just right."

She walked around the bed to her dresser and withdrew some comfy clothes. After slipping on her panties and executing some fancy moves to put on her bra, she peeked over her shoulder as she finished getting dressed. Noah was pouring the wine, his back to her. Oh, he looked really good filling up her space.

Shaking her head in an effort to focus, she stepped into yoga pants and a long-sleeved ribbed top. Both were in varying shades of purple, and among her favorite just-hanging-around clothes. She slipped on a pair of flip flops, and then peered into the small mirror above the dresser. She toweled and finger-combed her hair before turning back to her guest.

"I could use that," she said, coming up to him.

He handed her one glass, tapping it with his. "This is pretty good."

"It's made up in Lake County," she said.

"You go up to the winery in Lake County?"

"No way. That's all the way on the other side of Orlando. The town market carries it."

He took a sip and nodded. "I guess I'm going to have to get used to living and shopping right where I work."

"Funny, that's one of my favorite things." She took a sip and set the glass down on the small table. "Let me get started."

"Wait a sec." He took her hand and tugged her closer. He kissed her, sweet and hot and lingering. Pulling back, he shrugged. "I had to do that."

***

"I'm not complaining," Jessie said, her lips parted and glistening.

He smiled down at her before releasing her. "What do you want me to do?"

She arched a brow. "You're going to cook in my house, now?"

He raised his eyes to the canvas roof and wood walls. "Not exactly a house, Jessie. And I know what I'm talking about. I'm a builder, you see."

She smirked. "So I've heard. There's nothing to help me with, really. Maybe slice the bread?"

He went over to the shelf set beside the sink and found a loaf of crusty bread. To say the kitchen was compact would be high praise. Everything was Jessie-sized, but it was still comfortable to work in her space. She was mixing something in a bowl over on the table while he used the bread knife he'd found tucked into the one drawer of utensils. A couple of cutting boards were set on their sides up against some stacked pans, so he chose the wooden one and got to work.

"Thick, thin?" he asked. "What would you like?"

She glanced over her shoulder, biting her lip. "How about thick enough for a sandwich."

He nodded and cut, spreading the slices on a plate. By the time he brought the plate to the table, she had it set for two. In the center was a bowl of crab salad and some big lettuce leaves. The salad smelled fresh and a little briny, and made his mouth water.

"You're too good to me, Jessie."

She shrugged. "I always make too much." She assembled a sandwich with plenty of the crab mixture and several lettuce leaves and then set it on the plate in front of him. "Oliver will be bummed. I usually bring him any leftovers."

"His loss." He sat and lifted his glass of wine. "To my personal chef."

She shook her head at him as she took her seat. "Don't get used to this, buddy. I only make dinner a couple of nights a week. Otherwise, it's me and the Town Tavern all the way."

He waited until she served herself and then took a bite of his sandwich. Moaning softly, he chewed and swallowed. "This is the best crab salad sandwich I've ever tasted. And I grew up on the coast."

She took a dainty bite and nodded. "Fresh."

They ate and drank, and by the time he was helping her clean up in the tiny sink the open flaps set in the tent-cabin's gables showed it was nearly sunset.

"More wine?" she asked him.

"Sure."

They took their glasses out on the back deck, settling into the Adirondack chairs. She kicked off her flip flops and sat cross-legged on hers, cradling her wine glass in both hands. Her hair had dried since her shower, and now fell in a soft fringe around her face. She tucked a strand of it behind one perfect shell ear, and he was tempted to kiss the spot right beneath it.

He knew her skin was soft and sweet. Hell, everything about her was sweet. Not as soft as he'd thought, though. Her body was rocking hot, which he'd suspected but was completely confirmed when he saw her in her running clothes. Even now, in her stretchy purple clothes, she was sexy as hell.

"Here it comes," she whispered, her gaze fixed on the lake.

He turned his attention in that direction and nearly lost his breath. Pinks and oranges flickered over the lake's surface, sparkling on the ripples and spreading toward them. The cypress and live oaks framed the view, the Spanish moss hanging down looking like black lace as the sunset lit behind it.

"That, Noah," she said. "Makes all of it worth it."

"Worth what?" he had to know.

She flicked her gaze to him, her mouth thinned. "Deciding to make this move. Leaving St. Cloud and the life I had there."

He guessed she'd left more than just an apartment behind. A guy, maybe? The one who had scared her? Forced her?

"The sunset, the lake, all of it," he began. "It looks good on you, Jessie."

She smiled, her face turned to the lake again. "It feels good. Really good."

As the sun made its final descent, they both grew silent.

Sipping his wine, sitting next to Jessie, was probably the nicest way he'd spent an evening since coming to Cypress.

What felt like just a few minutes later, the sky was dark. Sunset was a memory, but the sounds of the lake lapping against the reedy shore made up for its absence.

Noah set his glass on the deck and sank back in his chair.

"Thanks, Jessie. For dinner and for sharing this with me."

When she turned to him, her eyes were wide and shining. "It's nice to have someone out here, Noah. It's nice sitting here with you."

She sounded like she was surprised, and he couldn't blame her there. He didn't know what was between them, but friendship and heat were all twisted together.

"Why didn't you come by Saturday?" he asked her.

Her fair brows rose a notch. "I didn't want to intrude."

He shook his head. "I'm not buying it. Ben and Tammy are your friends, too. You hung out with me and Max Friday. Why didn't you come?"

"I didn't want to assume anything, Noah. Not after Friday night dinner and definitely not after what we shared Wednesday night."

The light above the porch flicked on. It must be on a timer

as well as motion-sensitive. Her skin picked up the light, looking soft and smooth. Reaching out, he trailed a finger over her arm.

"I don't know what this is, Jessie," he began. "I like being with you. Hell, I like kissing you. Loving you."

Her pupils dilated at his words and she sucked in a breath. "What are you saying, Noah? This is just convenient?"

He let out a short laugh. "This isn't convenient. It's complicated as hell."

She put her feet on the decking and turned her body toward him. "Why?"

He stared into her beautiful face, seeing confusion and worry there. "We work here, Jessie. We live here. We have lots of friends in common."

"Those don't sound like complications." She shrugged, a sweet smile on her lips. "No one needs to know. I can keep a secret if you can."

A rush of heat ran straight to his groin at her words. "You're not the kind of girl a guy keeps secret," he told her.

She touched his hand, which was still stroking her arm, and grasped it. "Come on."

He let her lead him back inside, and to his surprise she urged him toward the bed. "Jessie, what are you up to?"

She pressed close against him, running her hands up and down his arms now. Her mouth opened and he drove his tongue inside, and it made his blood pound. Damn, he'd never gotten so hard so fast.

She pulled a hairsbreadth away. "Take off your shirt," she said, slipping her hands up underneath to urge it upward.

He obliged her, lifting his arms and letting her push his shirt up and over his head. She studied him, trailing her fingers over his abs and up to his chest. Her touch was light. Teasing. Her eyes were intent as she seemed to take in every bit of him. She got up on the bed and knelt to face him, coming up as he bent down to keep kissing her.

Leaving his lips again, she began to lick her tongue over his chest. She suckled his nipple, causing him to pull in a breath. Her hands were on his ass now, and before he knew what she was doing she had his fly unbuttoned. With one hand she pulled his boxer briefs aside and held him. He hissed as his cock grew harder.

"Fuck," he cursed softly.

She was studying him again, her brow puckered as she bit her lower lip. "I didn't know how to do this. The other night."

He swallowed as he tried to follow what she was saying. It

was tough, with her hands on him and her mouth a fraction away from his dick. "You don't have to do this if you're uncomfortable."

She threw him a smile. "You know what I'm really good at, Noah?"

God, he hoped it was this because he was about to burst just watching her. "What?" he managed to ask.

She licked the head and he nearly howled. "Research."

Taking him in her mouth, she began to suck and lick and nibble until he was having trouble standing. Bracing his feet apart, he put his hands gently on her head. He ran his fingers through her silky hair, over her supple back, as she pleased him with her perfect pink mouth.

He was close to losing it. Close to coming hard as she sucked him. Her hands were on his ass again, tucked inside his briefs as she took all of him. He threw his head back and let out a shout as he came, shuddering for what felt like forever.

When he opened his eyes he found her beaming up at him, her mouth shiny as she licked her lips.

"I guess that was all right?" she asked.

He tried to catch his breath, unable to keep the grin from his face. He brushed her hair back from her face and stared down at her.

"That was all kinds of all right." He bent down and kissed her. "Never let it be said that I don't return a favor."

Chapter 15

After Noah sent her reeling, the two of them cuddled under her quilt. They were both naked now, and his body was strong and warm against hers.

"I'd say we're even," Jessie sighed as she settled against his chest.

He ran his fingers through her hair again. She'd discovered that he liked touching her, even in this innocent way. True they were naked, but his touch was gentle now. All of that frantic motion and eager passion left a haze of comfort she'd never felt before.

"So, about that research," he began, dropping a kiss on her brow. "Do I even want to know?"

She smiled and ducked her head, her face hot. "Let's just say I saw things that are pretty hard to un-see. Learned enough though, I think."

"More than enough, baby."

The endearment caused a hitch in her chest. "I figured I had to keep up."

A laugh rumbled in his chest beneath her ear. "Mission accomplished."

Pride filled her. Not that she'd pleased him, although that

was pretty awesome. She was proud that she'd given more of herself without letting apprehension drag her down.

"You're so easy to be with, Noah," she said. "You make me feel safe."

He stilled, his breath held for a second. "Why wouldn't you feel safe, Jessie?"

She shifted, pillowing her chin on her hands stacked on his chest. His blue eyes were warm, and she took that as the encouragement it was.

"I had a really bad relationship. About five years ago. He wasn't good to me." She shook her head a little. "Or good *for* me."

"Is this the guy who forced you?"

"He didn't force me, like you're thinking. He was abusive, though. Verbally and, sometimes, physically."

She felt Noah's arms flex as he fisted his hands. His brow furrowed and his nostrils flared.

"How long were you with this guy?"

"Just about four months."

"How did you break away from him?"

She smiled ruefully. "He broke up with me."

He cupped the side of her face, stroking her cheek gently

with his thumb. "Not only was he an asshole, he was an idiot."

"So that's my sordid history, I guess," she said. "What's yours? I know you have an ex, but what was life like for a beach bum like you?"

He brushed his hair back from his face, wearing that crooked smile. "I guess I was a beach bum, since I did hang out by the water every chance I got."

She bit her lip and then shrugged. "I guess that's where you met Max's mother."

He shifted to sit up in her bed, bringing her with him. She toyed with the threads in the quilt, suspecting some grand sweeping love story was going to follow. Instead, he shook his head.

"No. Nadine, that's Max's mother, and I never had a relationship."

Whoa. "You never loved her?" she had to know.

"I didn't even know her. It was a mistake, but the best one I ever made."

"Max is pretty awesome."

His smile was wide now. "I love that kid. I just wish I could have him more than I do."

"You share him?"

"Sort of. Nadine has the most time with him. I'm hoping I can change that, now that I have a place here in Cypress."

"Would you want him full-time?"

"Honestly?" His lips thinned as he thought over her question. "I don't know if I could handle that, even if Nadine wasn't a great mom. I'm hoping to split our time, though."

"I bet you'll figure something out."

"We'll see. This Paul guy she's seeing gets to spend more time with Max than I do."

She could feel his frustration.

"My dad was always busy," she said. "He worked at the high school not far from our house and students were always coming by for help or guidance. But he made the time he spent with us memorable. Pretty awesome, actually."

"I'm sorry you lost him."

She thought about all she'd lost since her dad died. Her independence, when she was with Mitch. Her sister, when they quickly grew apart.

"I have a sister," she said.

His brows rose a bit. "Yeah? Are you close?"

Surprisingly, tears pricked in her eyes. All the pleasure Noah just gave her, and the intimacy of this particular moment, must have overwhelmed her.

"No. Shannon and I are very different people. We didn't used to be, but I guess we both dealt with our dad's death differently."

"Maybe someday you can reconnect."

She doubted it would ever be that easy. "I never say never, but I can't see that happening any time soon."

"Does she live around here?"

"St. Cloud, actually. We used to share an apartment."

He narrowed his eyes for a second. "Does she work at the End Zone?"

"Yes. Why?"

"When I went there with the guys last week, I thought I'd imagined that one of the servers looked a little like you." He smiled and held her a bit closer. "I just thought that was because I couldn't get you out of my head."

"Shannon and I were often mistaken for twins."

"I'd never make that mistake."

"No?"

His smile crinkled his eyes at the corners. "She's pretty, but you're fucking gorgeous."

The compliment, even with a touch of profanity, made her

grin. "Thanks."

"I should get going, not that I want to," he said.

"Mmm hmm."

"If I stay, we're going to do a lot more together."

"Maybe."

"I don't want to be the guy who makes you think you owe him anything."

God, he was so sweet.

"Speaking of owing, how about dinner at the tavern tomorrow after the tour."

"Yeah?"

"Oliver gave me a gift card for helping him with the Atkins sisters. I bet we'll need some sustenance, and maybe a drink or two, after touring the Chapman guys."

He kissed her quickly, then pulled back. "You're on."

***

"Meeting in fifteen, Pixie," Oliver said.

Jessie looked up from her laptop screen, blinking rapidly. "What?"

"Mr. Forbes called a meeting, Jessie." He crossed his arms. "This isn't like you. You usually text the schedule to yourself. And everybody else."

She nodded. "True. I've been wrapped up in the new specs for the green neighborhood."

"Those guys from Chapman Financial are here. Rick's been showing them around, but Forbes wants to introduce them to everyone."

She closed her laptop and gathered her notepad and pen. Pushing her glasses up on her nose, she stood. "Let me just grab a bottle of water and I'll meet you in the conference room."

Oliver nodded and headed toward the hallway. Jessie took a second to catch her breath. She'd had trouble focusing this morning, and she knew the reason why. Noah. Pleasing him had made her feel so strong. Almost powerful. And when he'd given that and more back to her? She'd nearly cried, it had been so intense.

As she shrugged on one of her new sweaters, this one in Wedgewood blue, she made her way to the break room. Tammy was there, holding two bottles of water.

She held one out to Jessie. "You'll need this."

"What? Why?"

Tammy shook her head. "Remember how you were when Noah first started working here?"

Jessie fought a blush, and hoped that if Tammy noticed

she'd think it was because of the silly way Jessie had become flustered whenever Noah was around. It seemed that every guy who came to Cypress was, as Tammy described them, gods among men. Now that she'd seen Noah up close and personal, Jessie knew her friend hadn't been too far off the mark. He was magnificent all over.

"Are these guys, you know, hot?" she asked.

Tammy gave a slow nod. "As the sun. And I can say that, since I'm married to the hottest guy in three counties."

Jessie laughed. "So are you saying I should brace myself?"

"I know you, Pixie. But maybe the meeting is a good thing. You'll have gotten a look at them before you have to give them their tour this evening."

"Yes, and thanks for that. Rick didn't want you to give the tour. You just had to go and marry a Chapman, didn't you?"

Tammy grinned. "It's not my fault Rick wants this tour to be Chapman-free."

"No matter," Jessie said. "I can handle myself."

Tammy narrowed her eyes for a second, her lips pursed. "Maybe you can. There's definitely something different about you lately. You just seem, I don't know, *more*."

"More what?"

"More you." Tammy tilted her head. "Maybe it's wearing clothes that fit you."

Jessie coughed. "Maybe."

"Let's get in there before it starts," Tammy said. "Come from a place of power."

"We're just meeting them, Tammy."

"These guys are from Chapman, Jessie. Hand-picked by Bill himself. Who knows what they're here for."

"That's not my problem, thank goodness," Jessie said. "I'm just giving them a tour."

"You and Noah," Tammy added. "Rick told me that. Are you going to be all right spending all that time with him?"

Jessie nodded, keeping her mouth shut. If anyone, especially Tammy, knew just how much time she and Noah had been spending together there would be no keeping their secret. And she was determined that no one find out what they'd been doing. Living in Cypress Corners meant that everyone knew everyone else's business. She wasn't ready to add any grist to the rumor mill, and she was sure that was the last thing Noah wanted. That might be the last thing he wanted but she now knew what the first thing was.

She hid a smile as she followed Tammy to the conference

room.

"I have to say, the townhouse looks fantastic," Tammy said as they went into the empty conference room. "You did a great job."

"Thanks. It was fun. Like staging, but for someone's specific tastes in mind."

"It doesn't even look like my place. You really made it Noah's."

"He said he wanted it to remind him of the ocean," Jessie said. "So I gave him beachy."

"That's not all you gave him," Oliver added as he joined them.

"What?" Jessie nearly swallowed her tongue. "What are you talking about?"

"You cooked dinner for him and Max Friday night," Oliver said. "Tammy told me."

Jessie managed to nod. Before she had to make some sort of excuse or explanation, Rick came in and they were soon being introduced to Bill Chapman's guys. Jessie had to admit, they were hot. One guy was tall and broad with dark hair and a chiseled face. His eyes were intense and she suspected his looks would be lethal if he ever smiled. The other guy seemed a little more easygoing, but that could be because he smirked a little bit. But as good-looking as they were, neither had Noah's golden hair or sculpted lips or crystal blue eyes. The way his beard stubble glistened like gold dust in the sunset. The way his throat worked as he fought for control when she'd…

"And Jessie will take over for me this evening," Rick said.

Jessie started as she found both guys staring at her. The stern-looking one gave away nothing on his face while the other guy's eyes twinkled like he was sharing an inside joke with her.

"I'm happy to do it," she said.

Twinkle-eyes, Eli, she remembered was his name, smiled while tall, dark and gloomy merely nodded. Everyone filed out of the conference room, leaving Jessie jotting down a few notes. She missed half of what was said, a first for her, but she knew just how to schmooze these Chapman guys.

By the time she got back to her desk it was nearly five o'clock. She didn't have much time to regroup and get ready for the tour, but she'd already met the two guys anyway. They were no longer a pair of unknowns. Besides, she knew that once she started talking about the green aspects of Cypress she'd just get into her groove and it would be as natural as breathing.

"You okay, Pixie?" Oliver asked.

207

She was shutting down her laptop and readying for the tour. "As ready as I'll ever be."

Oliver shook his blond head. "Did you see those two? Mmm, they were smokin'."

"And?"

"Just saying. Besides, if my usual luck holds they're both straight as arrows."

Jessie laughed. "I don't know if that's true, but you just let me know."

Oliver groaned and Jessie left him there, heading out to the lobby to wait for the two *smokin'* Chapman guys.

Chapter 16

Noah put his hand on the small of Jessie's back as the hostess led them to a table in the Town Tavern. The tour had gone much like he'd expected. Derek, the more serious of the two Chapman guys, asked a lot of pointed questions while Eli did his best to flirt with Jessie. Double-entendre and effusive compliments seemed to bounce off of her like bullets off of Superman. He'd had to bite his tongue to keep from telling the guy just where he could get off.

"We survived," Jessie said as they settled at their table next to the hearth. "What did you think of them?"

Noah thought before he ventured an answer. "They definitely have an agenda. They weren't going to tip their hands to us, though."

She nodded as she opened her menu. "I think they both rated us below their notice."

"Yep. Derek did seem like a prick."

"Derek?"

"The dark-haired one." He smiled. "You know, the one who *wasn't* undressing you with his eyes."

"You think Eli was checking me out?" She shook her head at him. "Maybe, but I think there's something more there, Noah.

209

He seemed like he was all light and laughs, but he was clearly thinking as we showed them around."

"So we did our duty, then," he said. "And Rick owes us big time."

"He paid it forward with me, giving me yesterday afternoon off."

He remembered just how great that had been, discovering her running toward him out there near the turn-off to her place.

"Mmm, yesterday afternoon. I gotta tell you, I'm a big fan of yesterday afternoon."

She sparkled at him now, her face a pretty pink and her eyes golden. "Stop that," she said with a smile.

"Your call." He folded his arms on the table and leaned forward. "This feels like a date, Jessie. Is this a date?"

Her smile teased him. "It's Oliver's treat, so I don't think so."

He made a show of looking around before facing her again. "You sure about that?"

"I don't think anyone here will think we're dating, Noah." Her eyes widened. "Oh, are we dating?"

"I think we just might be."

She gave a tiny shake of her head. "I don't know how I feel

about that."

He wanted to reach over and cover her hands with his, but seriously thought she'd worry people might take that the wrong way. Or the right way, since this did feel like a date.

"You know, I haven't dated in a long time," he told her.

"You?" She apparently didn't believe him, if the curl of her lip was any indication. "Yeah, right."

"Why would you say that?"

"Have you seen you?" She clicked her tongue. "Fair-haired god among men. Kissed by the sun."

He laughed out loud at her description. "You're killing me, Jessie. Is that how you see me?" At her nod, he looked her over. "How should I describe you, then?"

She gazed at him, obviously worried about what particular words he would use to describe her. Her worries were misplaced. His biggest problem was coming up with something to say that didn't sound like he was only thinking with his dick.

"Hmm," he began. "I think sweet, gorgeous Pixie with a smokin' hot body will do. For now."

"Noah." She was smiling, though.

The server came by with two glasses of ice water and they each ordered burgers. He chose a beer and she asked for a glass of Pinot. When the server left them, Noah broached the subject again.

"I get why you want to keep things quiet," he told her.

"I would think you would want that, too."

"Why would I want that?"

"Because of Max, Noah. Your son might wonder just what was up with us."

"He already is."

She gaped at him. "He is? What did he say?"

Noah wasn't going to tell her Max asked if they were getting married. He suspected she'd run screaming out into the night hearing that little tidbit.

"He asked if you were my girlfriend."

She seemed to tense. "Seriously?"

"I told him that you're my friend and you're a girl."

"I'm sorry."

"For what?"

"For making you come up with some story for your son."

"I didn't come up with a story, Jessie. I try to always tell Max the truth." He held up one hand. "On a need-to-know basis, of course. No need for him to know just what we got up to on my new couch pillows."

She smiled, her shoulders lowering a notch. "Okay, good."

Now he was at a loss. He'd never dated much. He hadn't had to, as egotistical as that might sound. He just seemed to take what fell in his lap. This thing with Jessie, though? He might have to pull his head out of his ass and actually work to not fuck this up.

After dinner, they stepped outside onto the wide concrete patio surrounding the tavern and Clubhouse. She crossed to a carved metal bench, this one resembling a dragonfly, and sat. The action made her skirt ride up a little, and he took a minute to appreciate her new work clothes. No wonder that tool from Chapman kept staring at her on the tour.

"About that conversation in there," he began.

Her body stiffened for a beat. "What about it?"

"Are we friends, Jessie?"

She ran her hands over her thighs, staring down at her toes. "I suppose so. I like you."

Her simple statement sent a spike of heat through him. "I like you, too."

"So then we're friends," she said. "With benefits, I guess."

"No," he snapped. Her head jerked toward him and he winced. "I didn't mean to bark at you. I just don't think of us that way."

She looked away again. "You think of us."

It wasn't a question, and he didn't really need to come up with an answer. He moved a little closer, breathing in her scent. Everything they'd shared the previous evening came back to him in a rush. Her mouth on him. Her eyes gazing up as she tried, and succeeded, to drive him out of his mind. And later, as he'd made her feel just as good.

"Come back to the townhouse with me," he said softly.

She looked at him again, her eyes huge. "I want to."

He managed to keep from throwing his fist in the air at her admission. "So?"

***

Her mind worked. Oh, she wanted to go home with him. It had been so nice being with him yesterday. Heated and close and not scary in the least. But sex? Because, she had to face it, they were going to have sex if she went home with him tonight. Could she let go of her fear and focus on Noah?

She licked her lips, willing her heartrate to slow. "Okay."

He smiled, slow and wide, and she felt the warmth of it. "Then, let's go."

She stood, fisting her hands at her sides to keep from

trembling. Taking a breath, she realized what was making her shake. It wasn't apprehension or worry. No. It was excitement.

"Oh, what about my Jeep?" she asked.

"I'd be happy to walk back here and get it later."

She shook her head. "I don't want anybody seeing it just sitting there in the lot."

Noah nodded. "Do you want to drive it over?"

"Yes, thanks," she said.

They walked over to the lot and she slid behind the wheel of her Jeep.

He leaned in to kiss her. "Promise me you won't drive home instead."

She placed one hand over his. "I promise."

"Park behind, if you like. On the driveway."

She knew he was giving her another layer of security, knowing a pink Jeep parked out front would tell everyone who passed by that she was at Noah's.

"I think I will, thanks."

He slid her that slow smile that gave her goosebumps in the best way. "See you a few, then."

They each drove to the townhouse. As the Jeep ate up the short distance from the Sales Center to his place, her mind worked in circles. Was this a good idea? Should she finally end her self-imposed celibacy with him? God, she really wanted to. She wanted to lose herself with him. Wanted to let go of everything she'd been carrying for way too long. The self-consciousness. The nervousness. The fear.

By the time she parked the Jeep behind Noah's truck on the driveway and shut off the engine, she'd made up her mind. She wanted Noah and he wanted her.

Noah was leaning against the truck, but he straightened with a smile on his face. She locked her car and hurried into the garage, throwing herself into his arms. Anyone might see her now, but at this second she didn't care. She couldn't wait any longer. She kissed him.

Reaching up, she framed his face and drew his beautiful lips to hers. He returned her kiss with obvious enthusiasm, and his hands were soon cupped under her butt as he lifted her against him.

"I want you, Jessie." He kissed her cheek, her ear, her neck as he slipped off her sweater. "Upstairs in my bed."

"Yes," was all she could manage.

He stepped back and grabbed her hand. Together they hurried through the kitchen and up the stairs to his bedroom. Her heart pounded harder now, and she was never more certain of this happening tonight.

She was soon on his bed, Noah kissing her again as he unbuttoned her blouse. Her cardigan was somewhere on the first floor and her shoes were at the bottom of the stairs. He kissed every piece of her as he undressed her, his lips grazing her shoulders and the swells of her breasts.

When he kissed her belly, she let out a low moan. The memory of his loving her with his mouth made her panties damp. Stroking his hair, she purred with growing pleasure.

"I can't believe you're here," he said, coming back up to kiss her lips. "In my bed."

He removed her bra and panties and then came up on his knees and stared at her. Hard. His gaze was hot and his nostrils flared. Every inch the hungry male, his expression nearly made her swoon.

"Noah," she breathed.

"Look at you, Jessie."

She was spread out on his bed and she resisted the urge to cover herself. "What?"

"I thought you were a hot little Pixie but, Christ, you're a fucking goddess. A fantasy."

217

His words of praise blew away any lingering doubts that might have reared their heads. "Reality bites," she said with a smile. "Take those clothes off."

He grinned and stood beside the bed. "You got it."

Pulling his polo shirt up and over his head gave her more than a glimpse of masculine perfection. His khakis were soon gone, and she guessed his work boots and socks too because he now wore only his boxer briefs. She could see him outlined through the thin cotton, and her mouth went dry. She ached for him, which surprised the heck out of her. He must have seen the desire in her eyes, because his face changed from teasing to intense.

He covered her body with his, tangling his legs around her before easing between her thighs. He felt so big, so warm and solid, that she couldn't help wrapping her arms around his neck and arching against him. His fingers began to weave their magic on her flesh and she shivered as her passions rose.

"Noah, please," she gasped.

"I will, Jessie." He kissed her, and then nipped at her lower lip. "I promise."

He reached over to his nightstand and rolled on a condom. She'd seen his cock before. She'd held him. Stroked him. Kissed him until he'd come. But to know he was going to be inside of her? She melted.

Coming over her, he began to enter her. She froze, suddenly anticipating pain. He must have sensed it, because he began to kiss and caress her again.

"Easy, baby." Reaching down between them, he teased and tickled her clit until she was aching to have more of him inside of her. "That's it. Take me inside."

Moving smoothly now, he sank into her with a groan. As he began to move, pleasure spiked over every inch of her. She gasped, heat flashing over her skin.

"You okay?" he asked, bracing himself on his arms as he held himself still.

His strength was coiled and held in check. Oh, it was sexy as hell.

She stared into his pretty eyes and nodded. "Very okay."

He softly voiced his relief and started to move again. Faster and harder than before, he brought out every sensation she'd ever imagined. The times they'd messed around at the tent-cabin paled when compared to the bliss of having Noah make love to her.

She wrapped her legs around his narrow waist, locking her

ankles as she arched off the bed. He took her hands from his neck and pinned them over her head. She gave into it, feeling none of the discomfort that had come before when she was with Mitch.

Noah kept thrusting in and out of her, bringing her closer and closer to climax as he moved above her. A wave of heat burst inside of her and she began to come.

Noah didn't stop moving as she lost herself. He simply cursed softly as he joined her over the edge a few seconds later.

"Jessie," he rasped, bending his arms as his big, beautiful body touched every inch of hers. "Christ, Jessie."

She closed her eyes and nodded, licking her parched lips as she made some sort of verbal agreement. He withdrew and held her closer now. His face was tucked against her neck, and he kissed her as his breath finally began to slow.

When he lifted his head she managed to open her eyes. "Are you okay?" he asked again.

His lower body was still holding her down but she didn't feel trapped. It was the same as when he'd held her hands captive. There was something about this particular guy that made her feel safe and secure. That was a big difference from trapped and afraid.

"I am." She licked her lips again and lifted her head to press her mouth to his. "And you know what?"

"What?"

She ran her hands over his arms to clasp them behind his neck. "We're going to do that again."

That startled a laugh out of him and he rolled over and held her above him. Her legs draped on either side of him and she felt him start to get hard against her belly.

"You got it, Pixie."

Chapter 17

Noah crossed his arms and stepped back to regard the house under construction. The block walls were secure, the roof shingled and the windows were being installed today. Soon the mammoth one-story would be weathertight and ready for interior construction.

This home had a more coastal feel to it, with clapboard-look siding on the front façade and deep eaves. It was a gorgeous design, and another reason he loved bringing Ben's vision on the paper or computer to life in the real world.

He drew out his tablet and pulled up the exterior paint package colors for this particular home. The body would be a rich blue-gray with creamy white moldings, eaves and columns. Since Ben ordered slate-colored paver tiles for the front porch and drive, the colors for the shutters and front door would be burgundy to tie in to the varying shades of grays, blues and reds in the pavers. It was going to beautiful, and building it as a model on speculation would pay off big-time for Forbes and company when the time came to market it.

He made a mental note to have Jessie stage it. She'd made his home feel beachy and he knew she would go to town decorating this place before they declared it open for business.

"That's an awfully big front porch."

"Yep." Noah lifted his head to see one of the guys from the design committee standing at the curb. "It's a pretty big house."

The guy was broad and a few inches shorter than Noah, and his Florida State shirt was stretched taut over his beer belly paunch. "What color are you painting it?"

Noah took a breath to hold back a sharp response. He recognized this guy now, and thought his name might be Jerry. He'd come around the worksites a few times before, asking questions about things that were none of his damn business. He also had a reputation for giving current homeowners a really hard time when it came to making improvements to their own homes. Even when Rick and Harmony wanted to change the color of the front door and shutters on their house, this guy made the mistake of asking Rick to jump through way too many hoops.

"The design committee doesn't have any input on new construction, Jerry," Noah said, keeping his tone even.

"It's Johnny," the guy said with a sniff.

Like it matters. Noah gave him a small smile. "My mistake."

"What color palette are you thinking of using on this house?" Jerry/Johnny asked.

"That's up to the architect," Noah said.

The guy frowned, giving his face a pinched expression. "We wouldn't want to see any loud or overly-vibrant colors in this environmentally-friendly neighborhood."

"Ben Chapman has never chosen inappropriate colors," Noah said. "The developer is very pleased with every one of his designs, down to the hardware holding the handle to the front door."

The other guy held up his hands. "I'm just saying."

"Don't just say, please." Noah stared at him until the man began to fidget. "Did you have anything else to say, Jerry?"

"Johnny." Noah just continued to stare hard at him, and the man shook his head. "I guess not, no."

The guy turned and walked away, still looking over his shoulder at the impressive edifice of Noah's largest project in Cypress to date.

"Tool bag," Noah muttered.

"What's that, boss?" Mike asked him, peeking around the side of the house at him. "Anything wrong?"

Noah shook his head. "Nothing, man. I'm glad I don't work in the home-improvement business anymore, though."

Mike just nodded and disappeared around the block wall.

224

Noah blew out a breath as he swiped through his tablet to find the rendering of the finished house. Coastal elegance, and it was as energy-efficient as it was beautiful.

"Stay out of my way, Jerry," he said to himself.

Jerry/Johnny was easily shoved to the back of his mind as he drove back to the Sales Center at the end of his work day. He'd given Jessie some space yesterday, which hadn't been difficult since she worked at the Cypress Institute all day. Maybe that was a good thing, since he couldn't think about Tuesday night without breaking into a grin. Damn, loving her had been incredible. And having her that second time? It had been even better.

He waved a hello to Sharon Walsh and went down the hall to find Ben in his office, just packing up.

"Hey, Ben."

"Hey, man."

"That blowhard from the design committee stopped by the model site."

Ben rolled his eyes. "Don't tell Rick. My big brother is just looking for an excuse to tear him a new one."

Noah chuckled. "I just wanted to check in before heading out."

"Plans tonight?"

"Maybe."

Ben shut his laptop and leveled a look at him. "With Jessie?"

Noah opened his mouth to answer in the negative, but shut it with a snap. "She doesn't want anyone to know."

Ben arched a brow. "Tell you what. Tammy and I were going to hit the End Zone tonight for wings. The little ravioli has been wanting spicy lately."

Noah nodded. "Sounds like your wife."

Ben grinned. "That's what I'm afraid of. Why don't you come by and maybe Tammy can ask Jessie? It shouldn't feel too date-y, right?"

"It sounds like you're familiar with this kind of play, Ben."

"Let's just say that Tammy wasn't hot to date me," Ben said. "Or to let anybody know we were dating, either."

"That sounds just about like my situation."

"Then six thirty at the End Zone."

"Okay," Noah said. "I'll just text her to let her know."

He drew out his phone and found her in his contacts.

What are you up to tonight?

Nothing. Why?

Wanna go out to dinner with Ben and Tammy?

There was a long pause and Noah looked over to find Ben watching him closely. "Hey, can Jessie ride with you? Then I'll meet you all there."

"Yeah, sure."

Noah quickly texted that info to Jessie and got a response in a second.

Good. He could feel her relief in that one little word.

See you later.

A smiley face came through his phone and he chuckled.

Just a couple of messages back and forth and he had a non-date with Jessie. He pocketed his phone and nodded to Ben.

"I'll see you guys there," he said.

Ben nodded. "Later."

Noah went out to his truck for the short ride home. He was kind of excited for this non-date with Jessie. He just hoped he didn't do anything to screw this up.

***

Jessie washed her hands in the ladies room at the Sales Center, taking a few seconds to fluff her hair after. She was meeting Noah for dinner, and with their friends on top of it. When he'd texted her, a surprise in and of itself, she'd simply

227

answered as any friend might. Then he'd asked her to dinner and she'd been frozen. Thank goodness he'd come up with the plan for her to go with Ben and Tammy wherever it was and meet up with Noah then.

"So." Tammy stepped out of one of the three stalls and joined her at the sinks. "Dinner with Noah, hmm?"

Jessie tossed her paper towel and faced Tammy. "It's not a date, you know. I'm going with you and Ben."

Tammy nodded as she washed her hands. "And meeting the guy there."

"Yes. So?"

"So it seems pretty coincidental to me."

Jessie blew her bangs off her brow and pushed the door open. Tammy followed her out.

"Not a coincidence," Jessie said. "If Ben told Noah to meet us there, who am I to argue?"

Tammy snickered. "Okay, Pixie. I'll play it your way."

Jessie walked down the hall to her desk and picked up her sweater and messenger bag. As she turned, she saw Tammy had grabbed what she needed as well.

"Where are we going, by the way?" Jessie asked her.

"The End Zone."

Jessie froze again. Shannon was probably working there. When they'd lived together her sister worked pretty much every night. She'd been avoiding anything to do with Shannon for a few weeks now. Maybe it was time to talk to her in a neutral setting. Shannon couldn't still be holding a grudge, could she?

"I haven't been there in a while," was all she wanted to say about that particular sports bar. She took a breath. "Shannon works there."

Tammy's eyes widened a fraction. "Your sister works there?" Her lips thinned for a second, and then she gave a quick shake of her head. "You know, I haven't heard you talk about her much in weeks. Not since you moved out here."

Jessie leaned against the wall behind her. "We lived together way too long, Tammy. It was high time I moved out."

"You sound like you feel guilty about that. Do you?"

Jessie took a breath. "I guess I do. Maybe a little."

Tammy touched her shoulder. "Listen, Jessie. I can totally understand the need to get away and live on your own. Take it from me. I have way too many siblings and too many nieces and nephews to count at this point. Family can make you crazy."

Tears pricked Jessie's eyes. "Shannon and I are two very different people, but we have our DNA in common. And I do love her. I just couldn't stand living with her particular brand of crap any longer."

Tammy gave her shoulder a squeeze and released her. "Enough said, Jessie. For me, anyway. Let's go get our hot wings on and not worry about it. You'll be okay, though? Seeing Shannon?"

"Yeah. It's not like we argued or anything. We just haven't spoken in a while."

"Fair enough. If you see her tonight, say hello or don't. It's your call." Tammy lifted her chin toward the lobby. "Let's go."

Jessie nodded and followed her out to Ben's waiting SUV. Thankfully, Ben and Tammy kept up a steady conversation for the ten minute drive into St. Cloud. She knew in her heart that Shannon would be working tonight. Her sister might party like she was seventeen but she never shied away from work. Jessie had to check that off as another thing they had in common.

Ben parked in the lot in front of the End Zone, and Jessie saw the usual collection of vehicles for this part of the rural city. Shiny hybrid cars, chrome-encrusted motorcycles and mud-spattered raised pickups filled most of the spaces. She spotted Noah's truck though, and thoughts about seeing Shannon faded to the back of her mind.

"No one will think anything about this, Jessie," Tammy said. "I promise."

Ben gave a short nod and Jessie breathed a little easier. "Thanks."

The three of them got out and headed into the sports bar. The place was dim as usual inside but the large dining room to the right was lined all around with TVs set high on the walls. The screens showed fishing programs and Ultimate Fighting matches along with just about every other sport ever televised. The scent of French fries and buffalo wings hung in the air, along with the ever-present malty beer smell. It wasn't unpleasant, but Jessie had made it a point to not go there for the past couple of months.

There were several families seated at a few of the wooden tables and booths, but it was a Thursday night. Couples and groups of friends made up the rest of the mid-week clientele.

A long bar stretched along the back wall and the wait staff buzzed around with round trays of food and drink. Country pop songs were playing on the digital juke box and the crack of ball against ball could be heard through the wide opening to the pool room to the left.

"Hey, guys," Noah said, walking toward the front door to

greet them. "They have a table for us over by the jukebox."

The server currently working the hostess stand gave Noah a perky wave and then walked ahead of them, swinging both her ponytail and her hips as she went. They were soon seated in one of the high-backed booths. Tammy had all but pushed Jessie in ahead of her and slid in behind, effectively making Ben and Noah sit on the other side facing them.

"Wing me, Big Ben," Tammy said with a smile.

Ben grinned in return and waved down the nearest server. Jessie knew that slight figure anywhere. The hair looked a little lighter and a little longer since she'd seen her last, but it was Shannon. She turned to walk toward them, freezing when she spied Jessie.

"Hey, sis," she said, crossing her arms. "Slumming tonight?"

"Hi, Shannon," Jessie said, her mouth dry.

Shannon's eyes, eyes so like her own, narrowed. "Nothing happening in Stepford tonight?"

Jessie shook her head. Ben looked between her and Shannon, and then spoke.

"A bucket of coronas and a plate of wings," Ben said.

"The hotter the better," Tammy put in. "How about a plate

of nachos, too?"

Shannon arched a brow at Jessie, who just gave a nod. Her sister's gaze fell on Noah, who looked at Shannon for a beat.

"Sounds good," he said.

Shannon watched Noah for a long minute, and then threw a smile in Jessie's direction. "Will do."

She walked away, her steps quick as she went behind the bar to put in their order. Jessie finally pulled her gaze away from her sister to find Tammy staring at her.

"You weren't kidding," Tammy said. "She looks just like you."

"Yeah," Ben said. "But, like, in an alternate universe kind of way."

"That's your sister?" Noah flashed a small smile. "I thought I was seeing things when we were here a couple of weeks ago."

"So you've said," Jessie answered.

Shannon came back with their bucket of beer bottles, and a couple of glasses of water for Jessie and Tammy.

"You'll need these with the wings," she said. She gazed at Jessie for a second, then lifted her chin. "You look good."

Jessie finally looked hard and long at her sister. She was pretty tonight in an edgy kind of way, but there was something about her makeup that looked a little off. "You, too," she said. "How've you been?"

Shannon shrugged. "Good. I let the apartment go."

That surprised Jessie. "Oh?"

"Yeah. I'm living with Rob." She turned and waved toward the guy behind the bar before turning back to Jessie. "He's the manager."

Jessie studied the guy in question, seeing a thick neck and big arms and a hard expression. "That's—" She stilled as Shannon tilted her head just right and light fell on her left cheek. There was a thick layer of makeup there, hiding what was a bruise unless Jessie missed her guess. "Shannon, are you okay?"

Her sister bristled, her mouth a thin line. "I have to check on your order." She disappeared into the kitchen behind the bar, the door left swinging in her wake.

Chapter 18

A different server brought their wings and nachos, but Jessie's appetite was gone. Noah kept looking at her but it was clear he was making an effort to talk with Ben and Tammy about Cypress and other safe topics. Jessie sipped her beer as she waited for Shannon to reappear.

"I'm stuffed," Tammy finally said, leaning back and resting a hand on the swell of her belly. "The little ravioli is officially appeased."

Ben smiled, reaching across the narrow table to cover Tammy's hand with his. "I anticipate lots of kicking tonight."

"Then maybe you shouldn't leave your dirty clothes on the floor," Tammy teased.

Jessie absently smiled, her eyes still searching the bar for her sister.

"Why don't you guys take off?" Noah asked. "I can drive Jessie home."

"Sure." Ben sat back and looked at Jessie. "That okay with you?"

Jessie nodded, her stomach in knots and her head working in circles. "That would be okay. Thanks, Noah."

Ben and Noah settled the bill, both of them waving Jessie

away when she grabbed her purse. "After the little you ate?" Ben asked. "No way are we letting you pay."

"Thanks," Jessie said, setting her purse back down on the seat.

Tammy shifted beside Jessie and gave her a hug, and then stood. "See you in the morning, Pixie."

"Yes," Jessie said. "See you."

After the couple left, Noah covered her hands with his. "I've been dying to touch you all night."

She freed her thumb and stroked it over the back of his hand. "I'm sorry I've been such a wet blanket."

"You're upset. I know you have some issues with your sister, Jessie. It can't be easy seeing her."

She blinked at him. "That's not it. Something's up with her, and I have to find out what it is."

His brow furrowed for a second before it cleared. "I'll wait here for you," he said. "Do what you have to do."

Jessie hoped her expression showed him just how much that meant to her. Standing, she eased herself out of the booth and went to the bar.

"Yeah?" Rob, the guy Shannon was evidently living with now, finally glanced at her. His eyes rounded. "Oh, shit. She wasn't kidding when she said you look like her."

"Where is she?" Jessie asked.

"What do you want?" Shannon said, coming out of the kitchen and walking up to stand next to Rob. "We're a little busy in here tonight."

Jessie wasn't going to argue about a Thursday-night kind of crowd right now. "I have to talk to you," she said.

She looked at Rob, who gave her a nudge with his shoulder. "Go," he said. "Don't be long."

Shannon nodded and crossed her arms as she turned to walk into the pool room. Jessie figured it was as good a choice of setting as any, since the sound of cues cracking into balls and the ringing of old-fashioned arcade games would give them some level of privacy.

"What's going on with you and Rob?" Jessie asked without preamble.

Shannon put her hands on her hips. "Rob and I are great. And what business is it of yours, anyway?"

"Is he hitting you?"

Shannon touched her cheek, and then fisted her hand back down at her side. "It was an accident. Is that all you wanted to know?"

Jessie reached out to grasp her sister's arm. "I'm worried about you, Shannon."

Shannon scoffed. "Yeah, right. Have you even called or texted me since you moved out to Stepford, Jessie? No."

Jessie flinched but she held her ground. "I left you a voicemail. You know, you haven't reached out to me, either."

"You made it pretty clear I wasn't welcome when you kicked me out of your little tent thing."

"You could have come to visit, Shannon."

Shannon waved a hand. "What's up with you, sis? That's the question, isn't it? That hot guy with you tonight. What's his story?"

"Noah and I are friends."

Shannon barked out an ugly laugh. "Friends. Like you and that dick Mitch?"

A strong point in Shannon's favor was that she'd hated Mitch on sight. Pity Jessie hadn't given her opinion a little more credence. "Noah's nothing like Mitch."

Shannon huffed a breath. "Good. That's something. Tell me, are you letting this one in your bed or are you still a frigid bitch?"

Jessie's mouth dropped open in shock. "Shannon."

Shannon held up her hands. "Look, Jessie. I appreciate the concern but I'm not your problem anymore."

Jessie bit back her own curse. "You were never my problem."

"Yeah? Sure as hell felt like I was." She pushed past Jessie toward the bar area. "See you around." She didn't look back.

Jessie stood there, her blood pounding in her ears. Closing her eyes, she breathed in slowly through her nose and let go with a loud exhalation. Her hands shook as she leaned forward and braced them over her thighs. Her eyes burned behind her closed lids.

"Doesn't look like that went well," Noah said.

Jessie straightened to find Noah standing there, solid and real and warm. Taking a small step, she fell against his chest and let him hold her. "That sucked."

He stroked her back, not seeming to care that she was losing it in a public place. "You're going to be okay."

She sniffled and leaned back to look up at him. "How do you know?"

He gave her a small smile. "I don't know, since I don't have any siblings."

"You see?"

"But I know you, Jessie. You're strong. You'll get through this and you and your sister might even work this out someday."

"Someday." She brushed at her wet cheeks and squared her shoulders. "She's a big girl, right?"

"Right."

"She has my number and knows where I live."

Noah nodded. "She can find you if she needs to."

"Exactly." She ran her hands up and down on his strong arms, which were still draped around her. "Let's get out of here."

"You got it."

She didn't catch a glimpse of her sister as she and Noah made their way out of the place. Rob was still standing behind the bar, watching them with a closed expression, so Jessie put him out of her head. Shannon was a big girl. She could take care of herself.

That didn't stop Jessie from worrying about her, but she'd give it her best shot.

***

Noah drove her back to Cypress, following Jessie's lead. They were quiet, and he could tell she was still upset about whatever went on with her and her sister.

As they pulled into the community, Jessie angled her body

240

toward his. "Take me home, Noah?"

He started to turn toward the far lakeshore but she put her hand on his hand.

"Your home," she said.

He nodded, correcting the wheel to steer toward the townhouse. They didn't even talk about her Jeep tonight, but he made a mental note to walk back to the Sales Center and retrieve it for her later.

After parking in his garage and turning off the engine, he faced her. He had trouble reading the expression on her face. Her brows were a little creased and her mouth was an even line.

"You okay?" he asked her again.

She nodded, facing him at last. "Yes. I'm sorry to be such a downer."

He drew her to him as close as he could manage with the console and gear shift between them. "Hey, you can let go with me, Jessie. This is a judgment-free zone."

She looked genuinely surprised, which only served to remind him that he had no clue about how to do this dating stuff. He wanted to figure it out, though. With Jessie, he thought he just might learn to work things out with another person for once in his life.

"Come on," he said, opening his door. "How about I find us something to eat?"

She nodded and slid out to join him as they walked into the kitchen. She settled on one of the barstools she'd picked out, her expression still pensive as he turned on the oven.

"Frozen pizza okay?" At her nod he rooted around in the bottom freezer of the big stainless fridge and pulled out a flat box. "It's not from the tavern but I think it'll do."

"It'll more than do," she said. "I really didn't eat much at the End Zone."

"I did all right but I was a little worried there."

"About what?"

"Every time I took another wing, Tammy growled at me."

That got a laugh out of Jessie, even if it was a small one. He found the wine bottle they'd opened the other night and poured them each a glass. He tapped his glass to hers. "To the benefits of dining alone."

She lifted her glass, and one of her brows. "Alone?"

"Just the two of us, Jessie."

She dipped her head, her cheeks warming to a pretty pink. "Something occurred to me tonight at the End Zone."

"Yeah? What's that?"

"I think we're dating, Noah."

"Oh, we're dating." He took a sip, and then leaned in to kiss her. "No question about it."

Her eyes were huge as he pulled back. "Are you sure you want that? It won't be a problem with Max?"

Noah shook his head. "Max likes you, Jessie. His mother dates, so he won't think it's weird if I do."

She nibble her lower lip. "But we both work here."

"So what?" Noah tamped down the frustration that was beginning to bite at him. "I know you've had an emotional night. Just know that I'm not going away."

Her eyes were clouded now. "Why?"

"Because I like you." He touched her face, feeling her soft skin with his fingertips. "I know you like me."

A flash of a sassy smile curved her lips. "You do, do you?"

He let his desire for her to show. "I'm pretty sure, Jessie. I have the scratches on my back to prove it."

That earned him a full, bright laugh. Worry seemed to fall off of her as she settled back into the barstool.

"Let's get that pizza cooked then," she said. "You'll need your strength."

As they shared their meal he marveled at this new

relationship they'd stumbled into. No. Not stumbled. He'd been attracted to her from the first minute he saw her in that big ugly sweater.

And later that night, when he had her spread beneath him in his bed, he couldn't imagine loving any other woman. Every inch of her body, every touch of her skin to his, made him burn hotter than he could have imagined.

"This is new for me too, Jessie." He ran his hands all over her body, every dip and hollow, as she moaned softly. "We'd be stupid to let this go." He kissed the side of her neck, breathing in her sweet scent. "Don't you think?"

"Yes." She gasped as he nibbled on her breast. "Stupid."

She was wet when he parted her thighs. Hot and slick when he slid two fingers inside of her. Every sound she made ratcheted up the pleasure as he settled between her legs.

"You want me, Jessie." He kissed her, still moving his fingers inside her. "Say it."

"I want you, Noah." She bit her lip again and arched. "Just you."

He managed somehow to grab a condom from the nightstand and take care of it before finally coming into her. This was different from their first time together. Sweeter. Sharper

244

somehow. More in focus even as the edges blurred until he saw nothing but her. Felt nothing but her body gripping him as he rode her.

She began to sob, soft sounds that told him she was close. Bending his head, he suckled her breast. As he pulled hard on her nipple, she began to climax.

"Oh God!" she gasped, wrapping her legs around his waist liked she'd done before. "Oh!"

He sank farther into her, feeling every tremor as she came under him. Finally giving in to his own orgasm, he held himself up on his arms as he let the pleasure wash over him.

"Jessie," he said, throwing his head back with a shout. "Christ, Jessie."

He thought she might have come again, he couldn't be sure as his own climax squeezed every muscle, before he let himself fall into her arms.

Her breath came fast in his ear as he pillowed his head between her breasts. Her scent was stronger here, her heart beating rapidly beneath his cheek as her damp skin drew his kisses again.

"Okay," she sighed, running her fingers through his hair. "You were right."

He tried to think. He really did. But her body still held him just right and they were still tangled up in each other.

"Right about what?" he asked.

Her chest hitched as she softly laughed. "I like you."

Something shifted in his chest. Something he'd never felt before.

"I think I could love you, Jessie."

"Don't say that," she whispered.

He lifted his head to find worry stamped on her face. *Damn it.* "I'm not that asshole who hurt you."

"I know."

"Do you?"

She nodded, bringing her hand up to his cheek. "Yes."

"Then know this too. I told you I don't lie. Not to Max and sure as hell not to you."

"Okay," she said again.

"I have to know if you're in, Jessie. Are you?"

Her eyes were shiny. "I'm in."

He kissed her then, savoring the taste of her as he reveled in the feel of her. Grinning down at her, he brushed her silky hair back off her forehead.

"I have Max again this weekend. Will you hang out with

us?"

She nodded, a smile teasing her lips. "I think that would be great."

He kissed her again and soon they started something he couldn't wait to finish. This time Jessie took the upper hand as he willingly gave everything over to her. Letting her take her pleasure on top of him was phenomenal.

Later, as she cuddled against him and their bodies cooled, he knew he'd found something wonderful. Luck had smiled on him again, giving him a fantastic woman he could maybe even see a future with. A doubt niggled at the back of his mind, though. He might have fallen ass-backwards into a relationship with Jessie but he couldn't help but worry that at some point his luck would run out.

And right now, with Jessie softly slumbering in his arms, he knew that if he lost her he'd never get this lucky again.

Chapter 19

"Now that's a smile I haven't seen on your pretty face before," Lettie said from her customary spot beneath the crepe myrtle.

Jessie couldn't rein in her happiness this Monday morning as she neared Lettie's table. "Good morning, Lettie."

"And just what has you grinning like that this morning, as if I didn't know."

Jessie lifted her café latte to her lips. "It must be the coffee."

Lettie folded her hands on the table, her sweet tea apparently as inconsequential as the seed catalogs she pushed to one side. "Mmm hmm. Seems to me a certain handsome man of significant proportions who knows how to swing a hammer might have something to do with this."

Now Jessie's face was burning hot, and she still couldn't manage to wipe the grin off of her face. "Lettie, please."

Lettie gave her a sly smile in return. "Jessie honey, you deserve whatever happened to make you turn that particular shade of pink. I believe I have a peony growing on the east side of my yard that blushes that exact color."

Jessie laughed. "I have to get to work."

"Do say hello to that sun-kissed man for me, would you?

Mmm, that man is mighty fine."

Jessie shook her head at Lettie and crossed the street to the Sales Center. That woman was incorrigible, but she was right on at least one count, though. Noah was mighty fine indeed.

The weekend had been more fun than she'd even hoped. Max was adorable, and Noah was great with him. The little boy was friendly and asked a bunch of questions that any six year old worth his salt might. Thank goodness she could simply wait for Noah to answer the tough ones. Like why the water from the splash pad at the park didn't just make puddles. It was clear Noah had some sort of engineering expertise to go along with his contractor's credentials. But other, softer topics, like why they didn't eat the catfish caught in the big lake, she fielded. Conservation was her thing, after all. Barbless hooks and catch-and-release were the standards for most of the year in Cypress.

On Saturday afternoon they decided to take Max to Old Town Village. She rode the Ferris wheel with Max and Noah and then let the two of them tackle the bigger thrills. She'd been content to watch as they took turns on the bungee-jump thing, and when one woman remarked about what a lovely family Jessie had she'd just said thanks and didn't get into it. The truth was, she wasn't sure where the three of them stood. It was way too early to even think about anything like family. Like permanent.

They'd even stayed as the sun began to set and the classic cars rolled out for their bi-weekly car show. Max, and Noah for that matter, had talked on and on about cars and trucks and all sorts of things that couldn't interest Jessie less. Still, it was fun walking around with them and sharing snow cones and those little striped bags of popcorn.

Sunday afternoon they went to Harmony and Rick's for a picnic, which had served to completely out them as a couple. Amazingly, no one there seemed the least bit surprised to see them together. And later, while Noah drove Max back to his mother's in Melbourne, Jessie filled up the big jetted tub in Noah's master bath and was waiting for him when he got back. A shiver chased up her spine as she recalled just how he'd reacted to her wet and steamy welcome.

"Hey, Pixie," Oliver said. "What have you been up to?"

"What?" Jessie stared at him. "Hmm?"

"Ho, you got some," Oliver said in a whisper. "So just what's up with Naughty Noah?"

Jessie gave him a slow head shake. "If you think I'm telling you anything, you're out of your mind."

Oliver opened his mouth to say who knew what when Tammy's scream from her office broke through.

"Oh my God!" Tammy cried.

Jessie and Oliver shared a look of confusion before hurrying down the hallway.

"Tammy, what's wrong?" Jessie asked as she skidded to a stop at Tammy's open door.

Tammy turned to face them, a huge grin on her face. "Nothing's wrong, Jessie."

Jessie saw then that Claire Chapman was in the office with her, and wearing a matching grin.

"Claire, what's going on?" Jessie asked.

Claire flushed a little bit, and Jessie could certainly sympathize with the woman's fair skin. "I was waiting until the twelve-week mark."

Jessie caught on then, although Oliver was apparently still in the dark.

"Twelve weeks?" Oliver murmured.

"Oh Claire, I'm so happy for you!" Jessie wrapped Claire in a hug. "Jake must be over the moon."

"He is." Claire's eyes were shiny. "We've been trying for what feels like forever."

"Oh!" Oliver groaned. "A baby! Seriously, Claire, that's great news."

"Thanks, Oliver," Claire said.

Jessie felt her own eyes tear up. She glanced over at Tammy. "You didn't know?"

"I suspected," Tammy said. "For weeks now. But this one wasn't giving anything away."

"So when are you due?" Jessie asked.

"Late September," Claire said. "Just a few months after Tammy and Ben's little ravioli."

Jessie's throat tightened as the love and happiness in the room hit her hard. This was what it was all about. Friends and family and babies. She thought about the weekend she'd just spent with Noah and his son, and realized that could lead to something she'd never dared to hope for. Her stomach flipped over and a wave of panic threatened like sudden dark clouds over the lake.

"Whoa, Pixie," Oliver said, coming to stand in front of her. "You okay?"

Jessie stared up into his face. "Hmm?" she managed to utter.

"You're white," Claire said, placing a hand on hers.

Tammy wrapped an arm around Jessie's shoulders. "What's

252

up?"

Jessie managed a smile, looking from one friend to another as she struggled with every thought hitting her at once. "Nothing," she said. "I skipped breakfast this morning, that's all."

Oliver gave a dramatic sigh, lightening the mood a bit. "Thank God. I thought you were going to pop out a little person, too."

Jessie waved a hand. "Not likely."

Tammy winked. "Not yet, anyway."

Jessie shook her head again. "I'm going to grab an energy bar from my desk." She touched Claire's hand now. "I'm so happy for you, Claire."

Claire was beaming all the way to the roots of her strawberry-blond hair. "Thanks, Jessie."

Jessie left Tammy and Claire discussing possible names as Oliver moaned about diapers and sticky fingers. She took measured steps down the hall toward the large office space that held the general sales desks. Once at her own desk, she sank down into her chair. Covering her face with her hands, she breathed in slowly until her head felt less like a balloon full of buzzing bees.

What was she thinking, picturing herself with Noah and Max forever? They'd shared one perfect weekend together. That didn't a future make, after all. As for her and Noah? They'd only been on a handful of dates. They'd only spent two nights together. Cold settled in her stomach, spreading through to her hands. Was she losing herself like she had with Mitch?

God, she'd thrown herself into that relationship with everything she'd had. She'd cared too much, and fallen way too fast. Shannon had warned her, but Jessie had dismissed her so many times that her sister simply stopped talking to her about Mitch. By the time it ended four months into it, Shannon was doing her own thing and Jessie was left alone.

It was a good thing Mitch had ended it. She knew that. Heck, she'd known that then too. She kept telling herself that Noah wasn't Mitch, and that the two men couldn't be more different. But what about her? Had she changed from that scared girl she'd been after her father died? That girl who'd been so afraid to be alone that she'd let a manipulative, possessive jackass into her life?

No matter how tempting it was to let herself fall for Noah, she couldn't do that. She would just take things slowly and force herself to keep things nice and easy. Wasn't that what every guy wanted anyway?

She was falling for Noah, though. That was obvious to her, if not to anybody else yet. How could she not? She knew something else was true, too.

There was no way she would ever lose herself again.

***

Noah took in a gasping breath as he fell onto the bed beside Jessie. He'd thought that what they'd shared Monday night at his place had been amazing but apparently he'd been out of his mind. They were at her tent-cabin tonight, and the sounds of the croaking frogs and buzzing bugs coming in through the opened flaps made soft music as he slowly came back to himself. Jessie was panting too, and her body was a little slick beneath his fingers as he stroked her skin.

"Baby, there are no words," he breathed.

She sighed, and then laughed a little. "You, without words? Amazing. Not even dirty ones?"

He barked out a laugh. "Jessie, you fried my brain. And just about everything else."

She kissed him on the side of his neck, doing that sweet breath-in thing against his skin that she sometimes did. "I'm worn out too, Naughty Noah."

He lifted his head, opening his eyes to gaze at her. "Naughty Noah?"

She leaned up on her elbows, quirking a half-smile at him. "Oliver pinned that one on you."

He winced. "Do I want to know?"

"I wouldn't."

"That settles it, then."

Shifting in his arms, she curled into his side. "I have an early tour tomorrow morning," she said around a yawn.

He shifted, cozying up into their embrace. "I thought you were at the Institute tomorrow."

"Derek and Eli want a real eco-tour and Ty asked me to tag along."

Something like jealousy licked along the back of Noah's neck. He hadn't forgotten how that Eli guy had flirted with her.

"They're still here?" he asked.

She nodded, cuddling closer. "Apparently Bill Chapman wants them to know Cypress inside and out before they head back to Boston." She snorted. "Like you could get to know this place in two weeks."

"If anyone can get them up-to-speed, it's you," he said.

The smile she flashed was bright and quick. "Thanks."

Then she frowned, pulling slightly away from him. "I should get some sleep."

"Okay, I can take a hint."

He was smiling but he couldn't help but feel like she was giving him the bum's rush. It was strange, since he was always the one to leave whenever he'd hooked up with any woman before Jessie, but he found he wanted to stay with her.

After he pulled on his briefs and jeans, he faced her. She was sitting now, her knees drawn up to her chest beneath the quilt. That slight frown still puckered her brow until she flashed him another smile.

"See you tomorrow?" she asked.

He pulled his shirt on over his head as he nodded. "Count on it."

The words meant more than any he'd ever uttered to a one-night stand. Damn, that seemed so far in the past for him at the moment.

Leaning down, he kissed her. Their lips clung for a few sweet seconds until he pulled back.

"Good night," he said.

"Good night."

He could feel her watching him as he stepped into his work

boots and walked outside to his truck. Something had shifted tonight between them. It was hard to put his finger on it, but it was like she was half in/half out. While he'd been loving her, she'd been right there with him. Hot and determined and eager to give them both what they needed. And for those moments after? He'd never wanted to let her go.

He drove back home, his mind still working even as his body was completely satisfied. It was too confusing to think about tonight. He and Jessie seemed in sync. In fact, he'd never felt that level of comfort and connection with a woman before.

He'd never been in a relationship before, though. It was possible that this was simply the ebb and flow of two people beginning to share something bigger than the two of them individually. Something that was probably normal for most of the adult population.

Maybe Ben could give him some insight. He'd said something once about Tammy not wanting to date when they'd first met. Just what had happened to change that for the man's wife, Noah had no clue.

Vowing to shelve the matter until tomorrow, he fell into bed. He couldn't get Jessie out of his head, though. God, he was so out of his comfort zone with this whole thing. Taking somebody's feelings into consideration wasn't something he really had to think about with guys. He made friends pretty easily but, now that he thought about it, he didn't really keep in touch. There were a few guys in Melbourne he used to hang out with, but he was damned if he could remember the last time he'd spoken to any of them. Maybe he wasn't any good at long term. Maybe he wasn't any good at making any effort to keep in touch.

"Maybe I'm just a shithead," he muttered, punching his pillow.

This relationship stuff was very involved. He could read a specification sheet and know precisely the amount of a product needed to satisfy a project's build. He knew how to get the best materials and still bring a project in within budget. This kind of thing was so far out of his wheelhouse. He was working without any plans on this, and he couldn't help but worry that he was going to fuck it up.

He was sure Jessie was worth the trouble. On that, he had complete confidence. They were creating a foundation as strong as any he'd built in his career. Firm footings. Sturdy walls. Weathertight fittings.

If anyone could make this project work, it would be him.

Chapter 20

In the morning, Noah drove over to the Sales Center. He knew Jessie wouldn't be there and, frankly, relief mixed with the disappointment he felt about that. He couldn't shake the feeling that she was pushing him out. Why, though? That was a whole different question.

"Noah!" Sharon Walsh smiled over the reception counter in the lobby. "You have to have some cake."

Noah blinked. "Cake?"

She nodded, pushing up from her seat. "We're celebrating this morning. Claire and Jake Chapman just announced they're having a baby."

Noah smiled. "That's great news. Wow."

"I know!" Sharon said. "Two Chapman babies are on the way."

"Wow," Noah said again.

He was at a loss to come up with anything else to say, really. When he'd been told about Max's imminent arrival, he and Nadine had been less than acquaintances. And, not to put too fine a point on it, there hadn't been cake.

"Go to the break room, Noah," Sharon urged with a frantic wave her hands. "Go and eat cake."

Nodding, Noah headed toward the break room. Tammy and Ben were there, along with the newly-expecting couple. Rick, Harmony and Mr. Forbes were also taking part in the celebration.

"Hey, Noah!" Jake said, coming up to swing an arm around Noah's neck. "I knocked up my wife. Have some cake!"

Claire groaned as she rolled her eyes, but the glow on her face was unmistakable. Ben and Tammy laughed and Noah joined them.

"Congratulations," Noah said, shaking Jake's hand before turning to Claire. "To both of you."

Claire beamed, her eyes sparkling. "Thanks, Noah. We're so excited."

Noah nodded, once more thinking about how he'd taken the news about Max. Somebody shoved a plate of sunny yellow-frosted cake into his hands and he took it automatically. Animated conversation filled the break room as the rest of them talked over each other.

"So what do you think about this plague of babies, Noah?" Oliver asked, sidling up to him.

"Two babies are hardly a plague."

Oliver threw up his hands. "Yeah, but it's only a matter of

time."

"Until what?" Noah arched a brow. "Are you and your guy thinking of joining the ranks?"

Oliver let out a hoot. "Todd and I are so not there yet, Noah. We haven't even talked about getting a dog together."

"Maybe someday, Ollie," Tammy said, swooping in with her fork to take a bite of Oliver's cake.

"Hey, hey," Oliver said, holding his plate away from her questing fork.

"Spoil sport," she grumbled. "You know the pregnant lady wants what she wants."

Ben was at her elbow with another slice immediately. "Easy there, sweetheart. Here's reinforcements."

Tammy threw her arms around his neck and gave him a loud kiss. "My man!"

Ben let her have the piece of cake and then turned to face Noah. "So what brings you by so early today, Noah?"

"They're painting the interior at the model today, so I'm going to give them a chance to get started. Actually, I wondered if you had a minute."

"Sure," Ben said. "What's up?"

Noah realized then that the rest of the makeshift baby party was quiet all of a sudden. Even the men were staring in Noah's direction.

"Uh, never mind," Noah rushed out.

Ben's eyes narrowed for a second before he nodded. "I'll be around for most of the day if you need me."

"Okay, thanks," Noah said.

Noah set his untouched plate on one of the round tables. He congratulated Claire and Jake again, said good bye to the others, and then headed back out to the lobby.

He'd been truthful when he'd told Ben he wasn't going out to the model this morning, but there were other things that could use his attention out in the green neighborhood. Standing outside his truck, he glanced over at the coffee shop. Maybe he'd get a cup for Jessie. He could use a cup himself, since he needed to do something to take his mind off of the winding track it had been on since going to that baby's-coming party.

Lettie waved to him as he neared her table. "If it isn't my favorite new builder here in Cypress Corners. How are you, Noah?"

"Great, Lettie." He stopped only long enough to give her a smile. "How are you doing?"

"Mighty fine," she answered.

Since her eyes were running all over the front of him, maybe he didn't want to know just what she might mean by that.

"I need to grab a couple cups of coffee." He lifted his chin toward the plastic cup on the table in front of her. "Can I get you anything?"

"Nothing, dear," she said. "Though I do thank you for the offer. I wouldn't want to put you to any trouble."

He found himself bowing his head at her. "No trouble at all."

She sighed, fanning herself with one of her seed catalogs. "A true southern gentleman. I must say it's some kind of wonderful to have your sort here in Cypress."

He smiled. "Are you saying you have something against those Yankee Chapmans, Lettie?"

She threw her head back and laughed, drawing barely any attention from the people coming and going from the coffee shop. That wasn't surprising, since every regular of the place had to be very familiar with Lettie Fairfax.

"Oh Noah Brady, you are too much," she said. "I do hope one of those coffees is for a particular pretty little Pixie we all know and love?"

His face grew hot. Damn, could the woman read minds?

"It just might be," he said. "I'll see you later, ma'am."

On his way back out of the coffee shop, he held the two cardboard cups aloft in Lettie's direction by way of salute before turning toward the Cypress Institute. The girl at the front desk, Becky, waved at him.

"Good morning, Mr. Brady."

"Hi, Becky. Do you know where I might find Jessie this morning?"

Becky nodded, holding up one finger. She spoke into the phone and then tapped on the computer keyboard before facing him again. "She's in the lab."

Noah peered off to the left of the lobby but Becky shook her head and pointed in the opposite direction. Nodding his thanks, he took the coffee cups and went down toward the lab.

The room was filled with file cabinets, glass tanks of plants and small animals, both in and out of water, and one long table with cushioned swivel chairs beneath. The table held several computer terminals.

Jessie was the only person in the lab at the moment, seated in front of one of the terminals. She was intently studying whatever page she had pulled up on the screen in front of her. Her hair was mussed as if she'd run her fingers through it several times this morning and her pink glasses sat perched on her little nose.

"Good morning, Jessie," he said.

***

Jessie looked up, blinking at Noah before sliding her glasses down a bit to peer over them. "Noah." Oh, he looked good this morning. He wore one of those Henley shirts she liked with a pair of khakis, and everything fit him just right. "What are you doing here?"

He held up one of the coffee cups he carried. "I brought you a caramel macchiato."

She couldn't help but grin. "Thanks so much! I've been craving something sweet ever since Harmony told me she was headed over to the Sales Center for some of Claire's cake."

"I saw that cake," he said.

"Claire made that cake," she said. "You've had her cookies. Her cakes are ridiculous."

He nodded. "They're pretty psyched."

"Oh, yes." She thought back to yesterday's revelation. "I'm so happy for Claire and Jake. They've been trying for a family ever since I've known them."

Noah took the lid off of his café Americano and sipped at it, his sculpted lips just caressing the cup. "They looked like they won the lottery."

She pulled her focus from his lips and took a deep breath of her sweet coffee drink. "Mmm. Yes, they're thrilled."

"You know, it's funny." He sat in the swivel chair beside hers and leaned an elbow on the counter. "I never planned or hoped for Max, but I can't imagine my life without him."

She pictured the tow-headed little charmer and how crazy he was for his father.

"You won the lottery with that boy, I think," she said.

"Thanks." His lips curved in a smile. "That's very sweet of you to say."

She sipped her coffee, bliss trickling through her along with the drink. It was almost as delicious as what she and Noah had shared last night. That was, before she'd forced herself to toss him out on his fine butt.

"So, last night," he began.

She stared at him, waiting for him to clarify his thoughts even as she worried over it. Had he felt bad when she'd kicked him out? He hadn't seemed too put out by it, but that might have been a result of the two orgasms he'd had.

"What about last night?" She ran a finger over the top of her coffee. "I thought it was pretty awesome."

He gave her that slow, sexy smile he usually reserved for bed times. "Thanks for that, too."

She flushed as she recalled the way she'd given him one of those aforementioned orgasms. "I believe I thanked you last night."

Chuckling, he drank more of his coffee. "And you call me naughty?"

"Excuse me. Oliver calls you naughty."

He held up a hand. "Please don't tell me that again."

They were quiet for a moment, just drinking and being in each other's space. She knew something was up with him, though. His eyes were clouded and his brows drawn just slightly together.

"What's wrong, Noah?"

"Why did you kick me out last night?"

The question was blunt and she resisted the urge to look around the room. She knew no one else was there, thank goodness. Still, his pointed question gave her no room to make up an excuse.

"I just thought it was for the best."

"Because of your tour this morning? I don't buy it."

She nibbled on her lower lip, knowing he deserved the truth. At least part of it. "No. I thought we were getting a little too…much."

"Too much, what?"

"Too relationship-y, Noah. It's not what you want."

His lips thinned. "You're telling me what I want?"

"It's what all guys want, right? And I don't want to…I don't want to be so involved."

He appeared to think her words over. Did he believe her? She'd nearly told him the real reason she'd sent him away. She was struggling to keep some space between them so she could prevent herself from falling too hard too fast. To keep from losing herself.

"Jessie, we're dating. Or we're hanging out, if you'd rather call it that. We're having a good time, aren't we?"

"Yes." She couldn't deny that. Having Noah love her was the best time she'd ever had. "Let's just keep it that way."

"Is this about what I said the other night? About how I could fall for you?"

"No," she lied. "It's just that you have your life, Noah. You have your son to worry about and the career your building here in Cypress."

"Yeah, so?"

"I have my work, too. It might not seem like much to you, but it's important to me."

"Don't do that," he said.

"Do what?"

"Belittle what you do. Folks here in Cypress have a lot of respect for you and what you bring to the table. They genuinely like you, Jessie."

She nodded her eyes pricking a little. "Yes. I'm making a place here, too."

"Do you like being with me?" he asked.

"Yes."

"Then why the bum's rush last night?"

She looked away, unable to face his beautiful blue eyes. "I thought guys didn't mind having an escape route."

"I used to map mine out before I even hit the sheets," he said.

She swiveled to face him. "But you didn't. Not with me."

"I like sleeping with you." He winked. "Even the sleeping part."

"Then let's just leave it like it is," she said.

He took another drink of his coffee, and then gave her a

short nod. "If that's how you want it, who am I to argue?"

The guy I'm falling for. Of course, she didn't say that. She couldn't say that.

When she didn't say anything in answer, he came to his feet. "I'll see you later?"

"Sure. And thanks again for the coffee."

He nodded again and left her alone.

She stared at the deflated foam floating on top of what was left of her coffee and sighed. It was better this way. For him, probably.

For her, most definitely.

Chapter 21

The eco-tour with Ty and the Chapman guys went as expected. Derek and Eli asked a ton of questions, which Jessie and Ty each answered in turn. She couldn't help but think about what Noah said about her place here in Cypress. She'd felt competent and valued on that tour. That was for sure. It still wasn't clear just what the guys were looking for, but when they'd passed where the Active Adult community would be built, they both straightened almost imperceptibly.

When she got back to the tent-cabin that night, she had a pizza from the tavern beside her in the Jeep. Noah was probably stopping by, and she would need her strength. For the passion, sure. But also for the act she planned to continue. Project keep-Noah-at-arm's-length. She was shocked to see Shannon's dusty Miata parked next to the tent-cabin.

Closing her eyes, she breathed in and prayed that her sister hadn't brought Rob or Billy or some other guy back to her house.

She stopped the Jeep and set the brake. Carrying the pizza, she stepped onto the front deck and pulled open the screen door. The main door was unlocked, Shannon apparently still had the emergency key Jessie had given her, so she pushed it aside and strode in. What she saw caused her breath to catch.

Her sister sat on the edge of the bed, her clothes rumpled and her hair a tangled mess. But it was her face that made Jessie's heart twist. Her makeup was smeared and the mark on her cheek was more pronounced. It was also clear from her puffy red eyes that she'd been crying.

"Shannon, what happened?"

"It's over, Jessie."

"What's over?"

"Me and Rob. My job. Everything."

Jessie put the pizza on the small table and then sat next to Shannon. "Everything?"

Shannon sniffled. "I have no place to live. Hell, I have no place to go."

"Did he hit you?"

Shannon nodded. "The other night, yeah. Tonight he just told me he was through with me."

"I thought you were living with him."

"I was staying at his place." She gave her head a shake, brushing her hair back from her forehead. "That's so not the same thing."

"But, wait. He fired you?"

273

She offered Jessie a watery smile. "What can I say? I'm as good at picking them as you are."

Jessie felt the sting of her sister's words, but she knew she was referring to Mitch. "You'll get over him, Shannon. You'll stay here and you'll get over him."

Shannon turned on the bed, hugging Jessie so tight she felt her spine crackle. "Thanks, Jessie."

When her sister pulled back slightly, Jessie brushed away some of her tear-streaked makeup with her thumbs.

"Go clean yourself up and I'll dish out the pizza," Jessie said.

Shannon nodded and shuffled over to the sink. Jessie watched her for a second and then grabbed her phone to send a quick text to Noah.

Change of plans. Sorry.

More than a minute passed before his answering text arrived. She filled that minute with worry over just what he might be thinking about her bailing on him.

Okay. See you tomorrow?

She wasn't sure if that question mark was intentional or not.

Okay. Good night.

Setting her phone down, she opened the pizza box and

shared it with her sister. While they ate, Jessie got the whole story on the trajectory of her failed relationship with Rob the Dick, as the sisters referred to him before the meal was over.

Apparently, he'd banged a few of the female barflies and thought there was nothing wrong with that. He'd started holding back some of Shannon's pay too, which he'd explained was to help cover for her room and board.

"I can't believe he did that. He really is a dick," Jessie said.

Shannon didn't smile but Jessie was pretty sure she appreciated her support. Her face lost some of its rigidity, at least.

Later, after Shannon was sound asleep on one half of the bed, Jessie had the chance to think about just what she was doing with Noah. She had to end it. There was no question in her mind now.

What Shannon was going through was the embodiment of everything Jessie worried would happen in her own life. Depending on a guy, for a job or a place to live, was just as scary as depending on him for her happiness.

Her heart squeezed as she pictured her life going forward. No more hanging out with Noah and Max. No more laughing and talking with Noah when they were alone. And no more of his loving her so well with his hands and mouth and incredible body.

Oh, his arms. No more would she lay in his arms and feel that contentment. That comfort. Tears burned hot in her eyes as she buried her face in the pillow and cried herself to sleep.

***

Noah brooded as he sat in the living room Jessie had decorated. His phone was tossed on the wide-planked coffee table beside the bowl of string balls or whatever they were as he blindly clicked through channels on the TV.

She'd blown him off. In a text, for fuck's sake. He'd known she was afraid of getting too close, and he could come up with nothing to argue with that. Except for Max and his parents, he wasn't close to anybody in his own life.

Should he talk to her? What the hell could he say? God, he was out of his element here. Specifications and materials and grade restrictions he could work around. The houses he built were homes for the families that occupied them. He knew that. He also knew that he had no fucking clue how to make a home for himself or Max.

In the morning he decided to forego a stop at the Sales Center. He wasn't a glutton for punishment, and he sure as hell didn't want to deal with being ignored or dismissed by Jessie in front of everybody there.

He'd dragged his tablet along, and would work in one of the model homes today. The big house's construction was progressing, and he knew he'd spend a fair amount of time there. It was getting close to the finish details, and it was on him to make sure that Ben's sketches were accurately brought to life on the inside as well.

As he parked his truck in front of the house, he gripped the steering wheel so hard the leather laces bit into his palms. The big truck from the cabinet company rumbled up behind him, and the sound of the air brakes broke through the fog. Putting on his game face, he shoved aside his confusion and went to work.

The kitchen would be the heart of the home, and like all the homes in Cypress Corners it would serve the future homeowners with comfort, style and convenience as well as serve the environment with energy-efficient fixtures. Cabinets of renewable woods and countertops of recycled glass in light and airy finishes would help bring the breezy, ocean feel home.

"Hey, Barry," he said to the guy stepping down from the big truck's cab. "We ready to do this?"

Barry, a supplier he'd worked with on a few houses before,

threw him a smile. "You tell me. Everything painted?"

"Everything's ready for you," Noah assured him.

He and Noah unlocked and threw open the back of the truck to reveal all the cabinets. Noah carefully peeled back the wrapping on the nearest cabinet, smoothing his hand over the smooth white Shaker-style door.

"Looks good, Barry," he said. "I'll get my guys to help unload and they can start this thing."

Noah headed into the house and found his finish carpenters busy attaching moldings in place at the baseboards. The white moldings were wide and crisp-looking, and popped against the cool gray wall paint. A darker gray colored the blank walls in the kitchen, and Noah knew the cabinets they'd chosen would look great in there.

"Cabinets are here," he said, causing heads to turn in his direction.

His guys moved to help the supplier and Noah picked up his tablet. He updated the cabinet install on the project schedule, knowing Ben would get the info as well. Going back outside, he helped bring in a few boxes until the countertops were exposed. Hopping up into the back of the truck, he looked over the polished surface of the nearest counter. It was a dove gray, with flecks of pearl and white and what looked like pieces of beach glass in pale blue-green. He couldn't help but think that Jessie would love this. He knew he'd have to call her soon about staging, but he didn't know which Jessie he'd get. Warm, funny Jessie who had an incredible eye and impeccable taste? Like the Jessie who'd decorated his home with confidence and style. Or would it be distant, hesitant Jessie? The girl who doubted herself, and him by extension.

Cursing softly, he stepped down and left his crew to work as he ducked into the completed model several lots away. One of the salespeople was inside thumbing through the information binder set on the work island, a woman he didn't know but vaguely remembered as having a desk in the big room where Oliver and Jessie worked.

"Hello," he said.

The woman, a blond with straight long hair, looked up at him. She was pretty, with blue eyes and a perfect-oval face. He put her age in her late twenties.

"Hi. I'm Bree," she said, coming around the island with her hand outstretched.

He shook her hand. "Noah Brady."

She nodded, flicking her hair over one shoulder. "Oh, I

know. I was at the meeting the other day."

Noah nodded absently. "You're working in the model now?"

She shrugged. "They want one of us in place every day, now that work is ramping up on the other lots. We'll give the inside tours."

He seemed to remember seeing a memo about that. "Makes sense." He held up his tablet. "I guess I'll work out in the screened porch if you're using the office."

"I'm not. Mr. Forbes asked me to set up camp in the kitchen. Next thing I know, he'll ask me to bake cookies."

He smiled. "I'll take the office then."

She returned her attention to the binder. Noah made himself a cup of coffee and took it with him to the office at the back of the house.

The room was backed by a wall of windows, and right now the view was half rolling grassland and half cleared lots. Trees dotted the view as well, and he knew most would remain in place to provide much-needed shade for the homes. The furnishings were done in what he guessed was light and fresh, with a gray parson's desk and chairs and pillows in yellow and white. One of those big white plastic sphere lights hung overhead. It wasn't his style, but he didn't care at the moment. It wasn't his house.

As he worked on specs and supplies for the next lot slated to start construction, a knock came at the door. Looking up, he found that Bree woman standing there.

"Mr. Brady?" she asked.

"What do you need?"

"Um, there are two men to see you out in the living room." She leaned in. "Those two men from Chapman Financial."

Noah nodded. "Thanks, but you don't have to work as my assistant."

"Oh, I'm not. I just wanted to let you know. They were making me a little nervous, just standing there and talking in half sentences."

Noah smiled. "No problem."

He followed her back to the living room to find Derek and Eli standing there. Eli flashed him a smile but Derek remained stone-faced.

"Hi," Noah began. "Did you guys need something?"

"Yes," Derek said. "We're heading back up to Boston but wanted to let you know that Bill Chapman will be in touch."

"With me?" They both nodded. "Why?"

"Just touching base," Eli said. "No big."

I'll just bet. "I'm assuming Mr. Forbes will be in the loop."

"Of course," Derek said. "And please tell that little sales person that she'll be needed, too."

"Jessie?"

Eli grinned. "Yeah. The pretty Pixie."

Noah somehow managed to not punch the guy in the face. "Okay."

They both walked out without saying anything more. Noah turned to find Bree wearing the same confusion on her face that he felt.

"What was up with that?" he asked.

"That was weird, right?" she asked.

Noah waved a hand as he went back to the office. He knew he'd have to talk to Jessie now. Something was up with those two guys and she was the one who gave them that tour yesterday. He'd just have to put the strangeness between them aside and talk to her. Keep it all business.

The prospect made him feel strange and out of breath. He'd fallen off one of the roofs he'd been fixing when he was a kid, and the breath had been sucked out of him. He felt a little bit like that right now.

He wasn't sure he could keep things all business with Jessie, but if that was how she wanted it, he'd suck it up and try his damnedest.

Chapter 22

We have to talk.

The text on her phone's screen might as well have shouted. She'd managed to avoid any thoughts of Noah for more than half the day, and now he was asking to talk? She texted him back.

Okay. Ugh, she was getting sick of that word. *When?*

I'll come by the Sales Center before five.

She wouldn't text him another "okay." She just wouldn't. *See you then.*

Leaning back in her chair, she took off her glasses and tossed them on her desk.

"What has your panties in a twist?" Oliver asked from his work station.

"My panties are none of your concern," she fired back.

He laughed. "True that. Seriously, is something wrong?"

"Nope. Just making things right again."

His brows rose as he leaned forward. "Yeah? Do tell? Does this have something to do with Naughty Noah?"

"Stop that," she said.

"Did something happen with you two? You know, other than the juicy stuff?"

"I'm not talking to you about this, Oliver."

"Suit yourself. I'm not one to pry."

"Ha." She softened her response with a small smile. "Whatever Noah and I had is over. It's for the best."

"Not by the look on your face, Pixie."

She straightened in her chair. "Don't you have work to do?"

Oliver sighed. "Always."

Jessie dismissed Oliver from her notice as she worked through her end-of-day tasks. Reviewing her schedule for tomorrow. *Check.* Cleaning her work station. *Check.* Packing her things. *Check.*

Meeting with her ex-lover. Oh, she could hardly think about that, but he'd be here any second now. Standing, she shouldered her messenger bag and headed out toward the lobby. It was probably best to meet this head on. He was waiting by the reception desk, talking with Bree who was covering the desk since Ty's mother went home around three o'clock.

"Noah," Jessie said.

He turned his head and gave her a smile. "Jessie." Oh, the way he said her name.

She fought its impact and merely nodded. "You wanted to talk to me?"

His expression sobered as he mirrored her act of

indifference.

"Hey." He nodded to Bree and gestured toward the front doors. "Can we talk outside?"

"Sure."

She held the strap of her messenger bag tight against her body as they stepped out into the bright afternoon sun. He urged her over to a bench set beneath a big live oak and she sat.

"So, what's up?" she asked.

His lips thinned like they had yesterday, and then he gave a shake of his head. "Those guys from Chapman came by to see me."

"What did they want?"

"Apparently Bill Chapman is going to be in touch with me." He waited a beat. "And you."

"Me? Why?"

"That's why I wanted to talk to you."

That's not the only reason, she knew he wanted to say.

"What do you want from me, Noah?"

She could hear the weariness in her own voice.

"I'm trying to keep this about work, Jessie. I would think you'd appreciate that."

She bristled but didn't argue. "Go on."

"Did they give you any indication during your tour with Ty?"

She thought for a second. "They seemed very keen to know more about the Active Adult community, but we don't really have any info on that yet."

Noah nodded. "There's big money at stake there, I'll bet."

"I can see why they would want to talk to you, but why me?"

He stared at her, making her heart race. "You're one of the best salespeople Forbes has, Jessie."

When she started to shake her head, he cursed softly.

"Why can't you see what's in front of your face?" he asked.

She pulled back. "What?"

"You're great at your job. You have friends here. Hell, you'd have more if you gave yourself half the chance."

She sucked in a breath. "I can't talk about this now."

"Why not?" He leaned closer, probably to keep their conversation appearing light to anyone who happened to glance in their direction. "What the hell is so important that you can't talk to me?"

"My sister is living with me now."

"What? Why?"

"She has no job and no place to live."

"I'm sorry to hear that, but isn't it just a little convenient?"

"For her?"

He cursed again. "No, for you. Now you have an excuse to push me away."

"Noah, please."

He stood. "If this is what you want, fine. I'm not going to push for something if I'm the only one in it."

To her surprise he walked away. Just like that. He ripped her heart out, threw it on the sidewalk and then stomped on it on the way to his truck.

She'd known this was the right thing to do all along. To end things with Noah before she got her heart broken. He would have grown tired of her anyway. Just like Mitch had. She wasn't worth fighting for. She'd known that, too. What sucked was just how much it hurt.

It wasn't until Tammy came and sat next to her on the bench that she realized over twenty minutes had passed since Noah left her there.

"Chin up, Pixie," she said, pulling her closer.

"It's for the best."

"Are you trying to convince me or yourself of that?"

Jessie could only shrug in answer, tears filling her eyes.

***

Noah's feet pounded on the pavement as he tried to run off his anger. What the fuck? Jessie had just sat there as she told him he wasn't worth her time. She had her job. She had her sister. She had her life.

He glanced at his sports watch and saw that he'd passed the six-mile mark. He was going for ten today. The sound of his feet on the road was his only music this evening. He hadn't even taken his phone with him, which might have been a little bit stupid. At least it was a cooler now. He squirted his water bottle over his head. Maybe if he ran far enough and fast enough he'd forget the way he'd felt when Jessie had simply ended things.

Why was he put out by it anyway? It was what he was used to. He never had to work for anything in his life, so why should this relationship be any different?

He pounded past the turn-off to her tent-cabin and kept his trajectory forward. The Active Adult community would be built out here soon, and if his strange conversation with Derek and Eli was any indication Noah would have something to do with it. That would mean spending his work days out here on the east side of the property. Close to the far lakeshore. Close to Jessie.

"Fucking fantastic," he grumbled on an exhale.

At least he'd have Max in April for his school break in a couple of weeks. When Nadine had told him that last night, the first thing he'd wanted to do when he'd gotten off of the phone was tell Jessie. She was so great with the kid, and it was obvious that his son was as much in love with her as Noah was. He nearly tripped as that thought bounced through his head in rhythm to his footsteps. Love. Fat lot of good that did him.

He rounded the scrub-covered end of the sandy road and headed back toward the town center. Once again he neared Jessie's turn off, and nearly strained his neck keeping his gaze forward. As he came into the more populated parts of Cypress, he kept to the bike lane on the pavement. There weren't many people out and about, since it was dinner time. Most folks were home or eating in the Clubhouse or Town Tavern. The coffee shop and bakery were closed and there was only the small light burning in the lobby of the Sales Center.

Cutting a path around the square, he passed the market and the ice cream shop. The place was so familiar to him now. It was home, but that kind of pissed him off tonight. His watch buzzed and he saw he'd completed ten miles. Pressing down on it, he paused and straightened. Taking slower steps, he placed his hands behind his back and took in deep breaths as his heartrate began to slow. He was drenched with sweat. He drained his water bottle and shoved it into the clip on his waistband.

The townhouses came into view a couple of minutes later, and he saw Ben sitting on his front step. He was tapping his foot on the walk and fiddling with his phone.

"Ben?" Noah called as he came closer.

Ben lifted his head. "About damn time you got here."

Noah rubbed his shirt over his face, and then brushed his hair back from his brow. "What are you doing here?"

"Tammy sent me."

Noah gaped at him. "Why? Or do I even want to know?"

"That depends, pal."

"On what?"

Ben grinned. "On whether or not you want to keep being a stupid dick."

Anger flashed through him. "Look, man."

Ben stood then, staring Noah down. "I know what you're going through. I never dated before Tammy."

Noah had thought about picking Ben's brain just a few days ago. Right now, though? Right now he just wanted him to get the hell out of his face.

"I don't want to talk about this," Noah said.

"You want Jessie, don't you?"

"Yeah." Noah didn't hesitate.

"You love her?"

"Love her?" Certainty filled him in a wave. She was sweet and hot and wonderful. He wanted her in his life and couldn't imagine his home without her in it.

"Yeah," Noah said again. "But she doesn't want me."

"Bullshit. She wants you. Tammy said she cried for an hour out on that bench."

"She did?"

Ben winced. "Shit. I wasn't supposed to tell you that."

"I don't understand then." Noah sat on the stoop. "Why would she push me out?"

"She's afraid, man." Ben sat back down beside him. "You know about her last relationship, right?"

"I know the guy was an asshole, but that's it."

"He treated her like shit, Noah. She doesn't feel like she's worth the effort."

"So she pushed me away." Noah groaned and covered his face with his hands. "And I just let her."

Ben was quiet for a long minute. "What are you going to

do?"

Noah lifted his head and looked at his friend. "Show her she's worth it?"

Ben arched a brow. "Are you asking me or telling me?"

Realization slammed through Noah, clear and bright as Jessie's smile. "She's so worth it, Ben. And I'm going to show her."

"Good." Ben grinned. "I'd give you a bro hug but you're a sweaty mess, man."

Noah laughed. "I have to go tell her."

"Now?"

Noah simply turned and started to run again. By the time he reached the tent-cabin he was winded but determined. He saw Jessie's Jeep and a Miata he guessed had to be her sister's. Whatever. He didn't care if they had an audience. He had to show her what he felt. Make Jessie admit what he knew. She loved him, too.

He stepped up onto the front deck and pounded on the frame of the screen door. "Jessie!"

The door was pulled open and her sister stood there. She wore a smug expression on a face that looked a lot more like Jessie's, now that it wasn't covered with makeup.

"About time you got here," she said.

It was almost the same thing Ben had said, and it was just as confusing.

"What?"

"Jeez, what did you do run all the way here?" She pushed the screen door open. "She's out on the back porch."

Noah stepped inside. "Does she know I'm coming, too?"

Shannon smirked at him. "Did *you* know, up to a few minutes ago?"

He found a smile. "No."

"Then get out there and make this right." He started past her when she held up a hand to stop him. "Wait a sec. Are you a dick?"

"No."

"Are you a manipulative asshole?"

He laughed a little. "No."

"Then you're better than our last two guys." She grabbed her keys off the little table. "I'm heading out."

She left, the screen door slamming behind her, and he went out the back door. He found Jessie curled up in one of the chairs, that big ugly sweater wrapped around her like a blanket.

"Hey, Jessie."

She started, turning to face him. "Noah."

There was a wealth of meaning in that word, but he was damned if he could figure it out. Her features were set, her full lips pressed in a line.

He settled on the chair next to hers, suddenly very nervous. "Jessie, I have to tell you." He shook his head and stood. "No, I have to show you."

"Show me what?"

He fell to his knees in front of her. "That you're worth it."

Her lower lip quivered and in that second he wanted to kill the guy who made her feel like she was lacking anything.

"Worth what?" she whispered.

He covered her hands with his, feeling how cold they were despite the warm evening air. "Worth everything, Jessie. I never had to work at a relationship, hell I never had a relationship before, but I don't want to fuck this up."

When she just continued to stare at him, he went on. "I don't want to take the easy way anymore."

"The easy way?" she asked.

He nodded. "Yeah. Coasting along. Taking whatever the tide brings."

"The tide?"

He shook his head. "I didn't have to work to get Max. I lucked into it. I don't want to luck into this with you. I want... I don't want to lose you because I don't know what I'm doing."

"I don't understand."

He was screwing this up and he couldn't lose her. He couldn't. He took a breath and jumped. "I love you."

Her eyes flared as her mouth dropped open. "You love me?"

He brought her hands to his lips and kissed them. "Yep. And you love me."

Her eyes swam with tears. "I do. I do love you."

His heart began to race. He grabbed her to him. "Thank God." He started to kiss her and she pulled back. "What?"

Her eyes were dancing now as she smiled at him. "You stink."

He barked out a laugh. "I ran here. After running ten miles."

She bit that full lower lip of hers and he wanted to kiss her again. "I know just how to fix that."

"How's that?"

Her head tilted toward the outdoor shower and he grabbed her. Peeling off that sweater, he found she wore her running clothes underneath.

She smiled. "Great minds think alike."

"Okay, great mind." He pulled his shirt over his head and grinned. "Can you guess just what I'm thinking right now?"

She peeled off her clothes and came into his arms and he knew this was right. This was real. This was forever.

And it was so worth anything he had to do to keep it.

Epilogue

"Jessie!"

Max's voice reached her and she rolled over to burrow under the covers. It wasn't as strange as she'd thought to sleep with Noah when Max stayed over. Of course, that was probably because his mother and Paul shared a bedroom now. That little revelation came out over mac and cheese during the last weekend he'd spent with them.

"Jessie!" the little boy cried, his mouth very close to her ear now. "Are you awake?"

She stifled a laugh. "Yes," she answered.

"Come on, then," he said. "Daddy has something for you in the kitchen."

She pushed her hair out of her eyes and sat up. So much for sleeping in on Sunday morning. And since Max would be spending a lot of time with them over the upcoming summer, things probably wouldn't change for a while.

"Okay." Swinging her legs over the side of the bed, she suddenly stopped. "Wait. He's not cooking, is he?"

Max giggled as he shook his head. "No."

Jessie stood and stretched. "Let me brush my teeth and stuff and I'll be right down."

Max nodded and was out the door in a flash. She went into the master bath and used the facilities. Brushing her teeth, she looked at herself in the mirror. A lot had changed in the two months since she and Noah had that steamy shower by the lake. He'd made love to her that day, showed her everything they could be and everything she wanted. She was in a relationship now, and she couldn't be happier if she tried.

By the time she went downstairs, Max was hopping up and down on his butt in one of the barstools. Noah was waiting for her, wearing a worn T-shirt and pajama pants. A sliver of skin showed just above the waistband, but she reined in the desire to kiss him right there. His hair was a mess but his eyes were bright.

"Morning," he said with a secret smile.

"Morning," she said. "What's up?"

"Do you notice anything?" he asked her.

She ran her gaze over him and then over Max before shaking her head. "Should I?"

"Over there!" Max said, pointing at the wall next to the fridge. "See?"

She looked and her heart tripped. There, hanging on the wall next to the metal N and M they'd bought on that long-ago

299

shopping trip was the letter J.

"You got me a J?" She clasped her hands. "Oh, that's so sweet!"

Noah shrugged. "I wanted to show you that you belong with us." She started to cry and Noah wrapped her in his arms. "Ah, baby."

"Why are you crying, Jessie?" Max asked. "Daddy said you'd be happy."

She sniffled and wiped at her eyes. "I am happy, sweetie." Looking up at Noah, she nodded. "So happy."

"Cool," Max said. "Now can we eat?"

Jessie and Noah both laughed and disentangled themselves. She popped two waffles into the toaster and they began to eat what had become their usual Sunday breakfast.

"I talked to Shannon last night," she said, passing Noah the syrup.

"What did she have to say?"

"I don't think she's going to like living out in the tent-cabin for long."

"No offense baby, but it's an acquired taste," Noah said, setting the syrup back on the counter.

She clicked her tongue. "She's not happy, though. I thought

if she started working here in Cypress, she'd begin to feel at home."

Noah arched a brow. "Do you think she'll leave?"

The thought of that possibility caused her belly to twist. "I don't like the thought of her moving away."

"She's a big girl, Jessie."

Jessie nodded. "I know. But Noah, we only had each other after our dad died. And I was a crappy big sister."

"You weren't." He stepped off his stool and wrapped his arms around her. "You had your own stuff going on, and so did she."

"Spoken like an only child."

He scoffed and held her slightly away from him. "I might not know what it's like to have a sibling but I know what it's like to feel responsible."

She glanced over to where Max was upending the syrup bottle over his waffles. "Yes, you do."

"She has to be responsible for herself. You have other things to keep you busy now. Me and Max? We're a handful."

What he said was true. It would be tough, but she had to give Shannon space to figure out her own stuff. She glanced at him and noticed that he had that mysterious smile on his face again.

"What is up with you, Noah?" she asked.

"Are you happy, Jessie? With me and Max?"

She blinked as she processed his questions. "Very."

Noah's eyes were intent on her. "Then stay."

She laughed a little. "Have you been able to get rid of me since Shannon moved out to the tent-cabin?"

"I'm not asking you to live with me, Jessie. I want you to marry me."

Her breath caught. "Marry you?"

He nodded. "Be my forever?

"Forever?" She swallowed. "Are you sure?"

He gave her that smile that always made her heart race. "Yep. Right, Max?" he tossed over to the little boy. "Don't we want Jessie to marry us?"

The little boy looked as surprised by the question as Jessie was, his blue eyes round. Then he gave them a syrupy grin. "Yep."

"Oh." She covered her mouth for a second, and then nodded. "Yes, Noah." She took a breath and sighed. "Yes, I'll marry you. And you too, Max."

Noah hugged her tight and kissed her brow. He gave her one

more sweet kiss on her lips and then leaned back with a grin. "I'm glad that's settled."

"Been thinking about that for a while, have you?" she teased.

"Oh, yeah."

She touched his face, rubbing her thumb over the golden stubble on his cheek. "I love you."

His eyes sparkled. "I love you, too."

He kissed her again and then made her a cup of coffee. They ate and laughed. They talked and planned. She'd been content to keep herself insulated from everything over the past five years. From entanglements, from relationships. She'd been content, but not happy.

Taking the job here had been the first step in breaking free, in reaching for her own happiness. Falling for Noah had been the last.

She still had her big comfy sweater, but she wouldn't use it to hide any more. She gazed at Max again, warmth filling her as she thought of having him as a stepson. Maybe someday she'd use that sweater to wrap up her baby. Hers and Noah's.

Noah showed her that day he'd run her down at the tent-cabin that she was worthy of love. He showed her this morning that she was worthy of forever.

She'd found her happiness in Cypress Corners with Noah. With Max, too. And this would be her forever.

About the Author

JoMarie DeGioia is a bestselling author of Historical and Contemporary Romance. She's known Mickey Mouse from the "inside," has been a copyeditor for her tiny town's newspaper, and a bookseller. A hybrid author, she also writes Young Adult Fantasy/Adventure stories, New Adult Romance and Paranormal Romance. She gets lost in DIY projects around the house and works out plot ideas during long runs. She divides her time between Central Florida and New England.

Discover other books by JoMarie DeGioia

The Dashing Nobles series, including

More Than Passion

Pride and Fire

Just Perfect

More Than Charming

The Gentlemen Undercover series, including

A Hero and a Gentleman

The Cypress Corners series, including

Finding Harmony

Taming Jake

Loving Cassie

Winning Ben

Showing Jessie

The Gifted YA Fantasy/Adventure Trilogy, including

Gifted

Braunachs of the Dell series, including

Luke's Gold

Patrick's Promise

Connect with me online

Twitter: https://twitter.com/JoMarieDeGioia

Facebook:

https://www.facebook.com/JoMarie.DeGioia.Author

Website: www.jomariedegioia.com

.